**"I'm Scott Lewis,"** he said when he came near enough to extend his hand.

"Becky Dennison." She drew a shuddering breath. "Thank you for coming."

Scott nodded toward the house. "Is Haldeman..."

"He's in the barn. I didn't touch anything." Fresh tears sparkled in her eyes. "Maybe you can figure it out. He's right outside the back door."

Scott glanced down at Becky, whose eyes locked on his, wide with panic. Steeling himself, he gave her a brief smile. At the doorway, he took a deep breath before stepping inside. When he caught sight of the body, it blew out in a rush.

Gashes punctuated Haldeman's bare chest. A sharp instrument had inflicted those many wounds. No matter what that woman out there said, this was no accident. Haldeman had been murdered.

**Books by Virginia Smith**

Love Inspired Suspense

*Murder by Mushroom* #63
*Bluegrass Peril* #82

## *VIRGINIA SMITH*

A lifelong lover of books, Virginia Smith has always enjoyed immersing herself in fiction. In her midtwenties she wrote her first story and discovered that writing well is harder than it looks; it took many years to produce a book worthy of publication. During the daylight hours she steadily climbed the corporate ladder and stole time late at night after the kids were in bed to write. With the publication of her first novel, she left her twenty-year corporate profession to devote her energy to her passion—writing stories that honor God and bring a smile to the faces of her readers. When she isn't writing, Ginny and her husband, Ted, enjoy exploring the extremes of nature—skiing in the mountains of Utah, motorcycle riding on the curvy roads of central Kentucky and scuba diving in the warm waters of the Caribbean. For more information visit www.VirginiaSmith.org.

# Bluegrass
## *Peril*

# VIRGINIA
# SMITH

Steeple
Hill®

Published by Steeple Hill Books™

STEEPLE HILL BOOKS

**Steeple Hill®**

ISBN-13: 978-0-373-44272-0
ISBN-10:     0-373-44272-6

BLUEGRASS PERIL

www.SteepleHill.com

**Printed in U.S.A.**

I will put my law in their minds and write it
on their hearts. I will be their God,
and they will be my people.
—*Jeremiah* 31:33b

## Acknowledgments

I'm thankful for the patience and expertise
of those who helped as I researched this book:
Mary Leigh Patrick, Michael Blowen, Paul Carter,
Trooper Ronald Turley, Anne Banks and
Phyllis Rogers at the Keeneland Library.
If I goofed on anything related to their areas
of expertise, it's not their fault.

I'm grateful to several people who have provided
invaluable feedback on this book. Thanks to
Susan Kroupa, Jill Elizabeth Nelson and the CWFI
Critique Group: Amy Barkman, Corinne Eldred,
Richard Leonard, Tracy Ruckman, Mary Yerkes
and Lani Zielsdorf.

Thanks to my agent, Wendy Lawton, and my editor,
Krista Stroever, who help me in more ways
than I can name.

Special thanks to my supportive family for loving
this book, especially: Christy Delliskave,
Susie Smith and my husband, Ted Smith.

And especially, thank You, Jesus. You know why.

## Dedication

For my aunt, Mary Leigh Patrick, whose love for
her horses is an inspiration.

# ONE

"Mommy, can we go to work with you and see the horses today?"

Becky Dennison licked a finger and smoothed an errant strand of Tyler's hair. "No, sweetheart. You have kindergarten today."

"Aw, man!" Tyler twisted in the high-backed chair and jerked away from her hand. "Do I hafta go? I got the meanest teacher in the whole world."

Becky carried her cereal bowl to the sink. She rinsed it and set it in the dishwasher, then returned to the small kitchen table where the twins sat finishing their breakfast.

"Miss Mallory is not mean." She gave Tyler a stern look. "You hurt her feelings when you told her she looked fat in those pants."

"But she did!"

Becky put her hands on her hips. "You don't say that to a lady. It's rude."

Across the table, Jamie's dark eyes, full of questions, looked up into hers. "You ask me and Tyler if you look fat all the time."

He looked so serious Becky worked hard to hide her smile. "That's different. I'm your mom. And Miss Mallory didn't ask." She turned back to Tyler. "She's a nice lady and a good teacher. If you would behave yourself like the gentleman I know you can be, you wouldn't get into trouble so often."

Tyler slumped in his chair, pouting. "Why can't I have Miss Peters? Jamie never gets yelled at."

Becky's gaze shifted toward the other twin. One of Jamie's hands busily played with a colorful action figure in a cape, the latest addition to his enormous collection of "men," as he called them. He fished the last bite of floating cereal out of his bowl with the spoon clutched in the other hand, and swallowed it with a loud gulp.

"Jamie, chew your food," she said automatically.

Tyler was right. Jamie never got into trouble at school. In fact, Miss Peters regularly sent home notes full of praise for his polite manners and excellent study habits. Notes from Miss Mallory set her teeth on edge. How could two boys who looked so much alike have such different personalities? Because they each took after a different parent.

Becky picked up Jamie's empty bowl and turned toward the sink, her back to the boys so they wouldn't see her grimace. Jamie was like her, quiet and introspective, except when his brother involved him in mischief. On the other hand, from birth Tyler had proven himself to be so much like his father it was almost frightening. He came into the world yelling and fighting, as though angry at his brother for being born first. From that moment, he seemed determined not to settle for second place ever again, and greedily demanded more than his fair share of everything—attention, milk, even space in the bassinet.

Becky set Jamie's bowl in the top rack beside her own and blew out a deep breath. She would not ruin this beautiful April day with thoughts of her ex-husband.

"You can't have Miss Peters because you have Miss Mallory," she told her youngest son. "Make the best of it."

Tyler folded his arms across his chest and slid farther down in the chair, his dark eyebrows drawn into a scowl. A typical Christopher expression. The resemblance between father and son struck her anew. In fact, both boys looked like their father, with his dark hair and eyes, his strong chin and chiseled nose. They were both good athletes, too, with tall, slender bodies that shed all traces of baby fat by their third year. Taking after Christopher in that respect was probably a good thing. She wouldn't wish her short, plump body and heart-shaped face on anyone.

Across the table, Jamie lifted his chin and smirked at his brother. "My teacher rocks."

"Jamie, don't be annoying," she scolded. He might be quiet at school, but Jamie wasn't a wimp. He could hold his own with his rowdy twin. "All right, boys, brush your teeth and get your backpacks. It's almost time to leave. Jamie, leave the men at home."

"Aw, Mom!"

Chairs scraped across the floor as the boys tumbled out of them. They ran from the room, and Becky swiped the table with a dishcloth, mentally planning her route to work. She had a couple of errands to do on the way this morning. She needed to stop for gasoline, and yesterday her boss, Neal, asked her to pick up some carrots. They had a tour scheduled at eleven o'clock, and the horses expected lots of carrots while the tourists gawked at them.

* * *

Forty minutes later, Becky turned from a two-lane country road onto the paved driveway of the old converted farmhouse where she worked. She noted with satisfaction the freshly painted letters of the wooden sign in the front yard: Out to Pasture, A Thoroughbred Retirement Farm. That faded sign had bugged her for the two months since she came to work here, and she finally took matters into her own hands and re-painted it a few days ago. It looked much better, nice, even. At the rear of the house she parked beside the boss's pickup, in front of the small barn where they stored supplies for their fifteen retired Thoroughbred champions.

She got out of the car and leaned against the open door to let her gaze sweep over the deep green Kentucky horse farm. Double rows of black plank fencing divided gently rolling swells of pasture. Heavy dew clung to the grass, sparkling in the sunlight on this crisp spring morning. She turned and looked across the road, where the mares with their foals were pastured. The babies hung close to their mothers today. Sometimes they ran and frolicked, and Becky loved to watch their graceful movements as they stretched their limbs and tested their limits. They seemed to know they were a special breed among horses. Thoroughbreds. Born to run, to train as elite equine athletes, and perhaps even to win that coveted Kentucky prize, a blanket of roses.

Becky leaned into the car and snatched the bag of carrots from the passenger seat. A muted bark reached her ears, and she glanced toward the back door of the farm-house that served as the retirement farm's office and founder Neal Haldeman's home. The wooden door stood open, indicating the boss was already out and about, as usual. But Neal's yellow Labrador retriever stood on hind legs inside the house, his front paws pressed against the glass storm door, barking. Odd. Neal always let Sam out first thing in the morning. Why was the dog still inside? Becky scanned the paddocks, but saw no sign of her boss. He must be in the barn. She slammed the car door and headed toward the house.

Galloping hooves thundered behind her, accompanied by a loud whinny. She turned to see Alidor racing across the turf toward her. Her pulse picked up speed, pounding in rhythm with the sound of his hooves. He arrived at the black plank fence, turned sideways and came to a quick stop.

Alidor frightened her. He was the biggest of the champions at the Pasture, and the meanest. No stallion was nice, according to Neal, but Alidor's fiery personality and aggressive behavior had scared even him when the horse first arrived. Becky stayed as far away from Alidor as she could, and he ignored her completely.

But not this morning. Alidor continued to whinny, his ears pinned almost flat to his head, his lips pulled back to show his teeth and gums. She had never heard that loud, high-pitched sound from any of the horses. Her stomach tightened at the urgency in the stallion's tone.

Surely Neal would hear and come to investigate. She glanced at the barn. Seeing no movement, she took a hesitant step toward the agitated horse.

"What's wrong, Alidor?"

Alidor tossed his head and pawed the ground with a front hoof. Becky took a few more steps. Maybe he smelled the carrots. Should she offer him one? Her heart thudded with fear. He had been known to bite, and was one of the stallions Neal would not let visitors feed.

Besides, he didn't look hungry or as if he was demanding a treat. He looked distressed.

Swallowing against a dry throat, Becky drew closer to the disturbed animal. She kept her voice low, the way Neal did when he talked to the stallions.

"It's okay, Alidor. Whatever it is, I'll find Neal and he'll take care of it."

As she neared the fence, she could see the rear of the barn. The back door stood open.

"Neal?" she called in that direction. "Something's wrong with Alidor. Are you in there?"

Nothing.

In the next paddock, Rusty Racer ran to the nearest corner and took up Alidor's cry. And behind Alidor's paddock, Founder's Fortune also began to call out in a loud whinny. Ten feet in front of her Alidor tossed his head repeatedly, white showing all around the intense dark depths of his eye.

The skin on her neck prickled at the sound in stereo. She'd only worked at the Pasture for two months, and she had never seen the horses act this way. Whatever was wrong with Alidor was getting to the others, as well, and she didn't have a clue what to do. Where was Neal?

"Neal!" Her voice, sharp with worry, sliced through the cool morning air like a blade.

His cell phone. Yes, that's what she'd do, she'd call his cell phone. She ran toward the barn. That extension was closer than the phone in the office. Alidor trotted along the fence, keeping pace with her, whinnying as he ran.

Rounding the corner, she shot through the open barn door. Inside, she tripped over something and landed facedown on the dirt floor with a hard thud. The bag of carrots flew out of her hand.

"What in the world?" She rolled over to see what had tripped her.

And screamed.

Neal lay in the dust, a pool of dark liquid beneath his head.

Outside the barn, Alidor and the other horses fell silent.

# TWO

Scott Lewis paused, his pitchfork full of manure-laden straw. What was that noise? It sounded like a scream in the distance, coming from the direction of the Pasture. He strained his ears to filter through the normal morning sounds of the farm. One of the stallions over there had been agitated all morning, but Scott knew Neal Haldeman could handle it.

The horse was quiet now, and he didn't hear anything else. The scream probably came from one of the peacocks over at the Hart place down the road. Pesky nuisances.

Scott went back to his chore. Mucking stalls wasn't part of his job description as assistant manager at Shady Acres farm, but he took pleasure in the mundane task and gave the boys a hand every so often. He enjoyed the chance to stretch his muscles, and the earthy smell of the barn brought back vivid memories of performing this same task as a boy alongside his father. Horse manure did not stink, not like cattle or pigs. Instead, the rich odor, reminiscent of sweet grasses, fertile soil and horse sweat, tickled his nostrils and settled a sense of contentment deep inside.

The phone on the far wall, an extension of Shady Acres' private line, dinged once. In the next instant, the cell phone on Scott's belt vibrated. Scott sighed. Marion over in the office must have forgotten to take it off forward when she came to work this morning.

He unclipped the phone and looked at the caller ID display. Uh-oh. Out to Pasture. His gaze went automatically through the wide-open barn doors and across the acres of fencing in the direction of the retirement farm. He flipped the cover open.

"Lewis here."

"H-hello? Is this M-Mr. Courtney?"

The voice on the other end was female, and tearful. Scott's grip on the phone tightened. Maybe that wasn't a peacock's scream after all.

"No, this is Scott Lewis, Lee Courtney's assistant manager. Can I help you with something?"

"I d-don't know. It's Neal. He's…he's dead!"

Her voice rose into a high-pitched sob. Scott's jaw went slack. Haldeman dead?

"How?"

The woman gasped a few shuddering breaths. "Some kind of accident, I think. There's a lot of blood. I called 9-1-1, but the horses…I don't know what to do."

Scott remembered now. Haldeman had hired a woman over at the Pasture not long ago, someone to answer the phone and schedule appointments, things like that. Zach Garrett, Scott's boss, made a sly comment at the time that she must be one fantastic secretary, because she didn't know a thing about Thoroughbreds. Knowing Haldeman's reputation with the ladies, Scott figured the woman's qualifications probably had nothing to do with horses.

"I'll be right over," he said into the phone.

"But Mr. Courtney should be told."

"I'll call him."

\* \* \*

Minutes later, Scott turned the farm truck into the driveway of the Pasture. Sirens wailed in the distance. You had to hand it to Davidson County EMS. They were certainly on the ball.

He pulled the truck onto the grass in front of the house. A parade of official vehicles was sure to crowd the driveway soon. He closed his eyes and spoke in a low voice. "Lord, this is gonna be a zoo. Help me see what needs to be done, and give me strength to do it. Amen."

He slammed the door and jogged through the damp grass toward the rear of the house. The stallions in the nearby paddocks were all in distant corners, as far from the house as they could get. They stood still, heads and ears lowered. Horses were smarter than most humans, in Scott's opinion, and definitely more astute. No doubt they sensed the tragedy.

When he rounded the corner, the door of an old red Chevy opened and a woman climbed out. She wasn't tall, probably wouldn't come up higher than his chin. Her light brown hair formed a widow's peak in the center of her forehead and hung in soft curls around her shoulders, giving her round face a heart-shaped look. Dirt stained her elbows and smeared the front of her white blouse, along with a few spots of what looked like dried blood.

She stared at him with wide eyes, and as he drew closer he saw dark smears of mascara beneath them. He steeled himself. Crying females always got to him.

"I'm Scott Lewis," he said when he came near enough to extend his hand.

Hers felt soft and warm, and his calloused mitt engulfed her dainty fingers. Tears marked the face she tilted up toward his. She sure didn't look the way he expected. Haldeman normally went for the flashier type.

"Becky Dennison." She drew a shuddering breath. "Thank you for coming."

"Lee will be here soon." Scott nodded toward the house. "Is Haldeman…?"

Becky's shoulders quaked. "He's in the barn. I decided to wait in my car. I didn't want to disturb anything."

"That's good. I'm sure the police will want to look around. Any idea what happened?"

She shook her head, swallowing. Fresh tears sparkled in her eyes, highlighting green flecks among the brown. She had eyes like Megan. Scott looked away, his throat suddenly tight.

"Maybe you can figure it out." Her voice trembled. "He's right inside the back door."

The last thing Scott wanted to do was look at Haldeman's dead body. "Let's wait for the experts."

The scream of sirens grew louder as a fire truck and an ambulance topped a hill and rounded a curve down the road, just beyond neighbor Justin Hart's farm. Within seconds the driveway was full, and Scott fought the urge to imitate Becky and cover his ears from the piercing noise. Behind them, the horses whinnied at the unfamiliar sound. Uniformed men leaped from the vehicles, and thankfully, the sirens stopped. Red lights, dimmed by the brilliance of the morning sun, flashed rhythmically against the white house.

Emergency bags in hand, the EMTs headed toward the two of them. Scott glanced down at Becky, whose eyes locked onto his, wide with panic. Apparently, she didn't want to see Haldeman's body again, either.

Steeling himself, he gave her a brief smile and spoke to the men. "He's out here, guys. Follow me."

He led the troop around the barn. At the doorway, he took a deep breath before stepping inside. When he caught sight of Haldeman, it blew out in a rush.

The man lay faceup on the floor wearing a pair of jeans, an open flannel work shirt and moccasin-style bedroom slippers. His body bore evidence of a struggle—bloody gashes punctuated his bare chest. Thick, dark blood covered one side of his neck and matted the hair above one ear. A sharp instrument inflicted those wounds. A knife?

The group of officials stopped beside Scott, all of them staring. One EMT approached the body and knelt to press a finger against Haldeman's neck, taking care not to disturb the pooled blood beneath him. A shake of the man's head provided the unnecessary verification of Haldeman's death.

A bitter taste assaulted Scott's mouth. No matter what that woman out there said, this was no accident. Haldeman had been murdered.

# THREE

It was a bad dream, a nightmare. Becky leaned against her car, trying to stay out of the way of the army of officials swarming toward the barn. After the ambulance and fire truck, three sheriff's vehicles arrived along with two more fire trucks, and then the sheriff himself.

"Ridiculous, isn't it?"

She tilted her head to look up at Scott Lewis. He stood, arms folded across his chest, watching the deputies wrap yellow tape all around the barn.

"What?"

He shook his head. "I was just thinking of the cost of sending all these people out here. How much do you suppose the accumulated salaries would come to?"

Becky shook her head. Strange man. What in the world would make him think of salaries at a time like this? "I really don't know."

"And most of them aren't doing a thing. Just standing around, waiting, like us."

"What are we waiting for, anyway?" Becky rubbed her hands on her arms, cold despite her sweater. "Why don't they question me?"

"Sheriff said we're waiting for the state police." Scott

must have noticed her shiver, because he said, "Here, stand over here in the sun. It'll warm you up in no time."

She stood where he indicated, and warm rays penetrated the chill. Smiling her thanks, she studied him. His skin was permanently tanned, the color of a man who worked in the sun every day of his life. Dark hair, combed straight back from his forehead, brushed at the tips of his ears and flipped out just above his collar. And muscles! Here was a man who wasn't afraid of hard work, and proved it every day. The merest hint of a cleft divided his narrow chin. She'd always been a sucker for men with cleft chins.

*Get a grip, woman! Your boss's dead body is no more than fifty feet away and you're checking out the guy next door. How gruesome is that?*

Inappropriate or not, her breath came shallow as she looked into dark brown eyes framed by lines that deepened into creases when he returned her smile.

He could use a shave, though.

"Here's Lee." Scott's voice cut into her thoughts and she looked quickly away, face warming. Had she been staring?

A silver Lexus slowed in front of the overcrowded driveway and then rolled into the grass along the front fence. Mr. Courtney emerged and walked with a confident step toward her. Zach Garrett, the manager of Shady Acres horse farm, got out of the passenger seat and followed the older man.

Thank goodness Mr. Courtney was finally here. He held both hands out toward Becky, and she restrained herself from running into them. Besides being a familiar face, his distinguished gray hair and easy confidence made him seem at the moment like a long lost friend. But he was a rich horse breeder, and the owner of the land leased by Out to Pasture to house the retired champions. He was also on the Pasture's board. He might be familiar, but he was definitely not the kind of man she should hug.

Instead, Becky stepped forward, grasped both of his hands in hers and squeezed. "Thank you so much for coming, Mr. Courtney. It's terrible."

"My dear, I know it is. You're in shock, as we all are." He looked past her shoulder at Scott. "Have you seen him?"

"Yes, sir. Looks like there was a fight, and he put up quite a struggle."

The sheriff approached the group and dipped his forehead toward Mr. Courtney. "Morning, Lee."

The two men shook hands. "Frank, I'm glad you're here. You can tell us what's happening."

Sheriff Holmes shook his head. "Haldeman's dead. That's about all I know at this point."

Zach gave a snort. "Betcha somebody's husband finally caught up with him."

Beside her, Scott grunted. "The man's dead, Zach. Show a little respect."

Zach cocked his head to one side. "Just statin' the facts as I know 'em."

Becky's gaze flew toward him. She had met the Shady Acres manager once or twice. He reminded her of Daddy, with his salt-and-pepper hair and no-nonsense manner.

Color rose up Zach's neck, and he pushed the cowboy hat to the back of his head with a finger. "Sorry, ma'am," he mumbled.

"That dog's going nuts." Scott looked toward the house, and Becky flushed with guilt. She had forgotten all about Sam.

"I'm sure he needs to go out," she said. "I was afraid he would disturb, uh, Neal, so I didn't release him when I got here."

"Put him on a leash," advised the sheriff. "He might get in the way of the investigators when they arrive."

Scott shook his head. "He doesn't need a leash. I'll watch him. Sam and I are buddies."

With a nod toward Becky and the men, he walked off in the direction of the house where poor Sam, trapped behind the storm door, had lifted his head and begun to howl.

"Investigators?" Mr. Courtney looked at the sheriff.

Sheriff Holmes nodded. "Soon as we ruled it a homicide, we called in the state boys. They ought to be here soon."

"That's probably them now," said Zach.

Becky followed his gaze. A dark blue sedan rolled to a stop behind the Lexus. A man in a gray suit got out of the driver's side, and a tall man in a state police uniform stood on the other side.

Becky recognized the state trooper. Jeff Whitley. He attended Grace Community Church and dated Becky's friend Amber. If Jeff had been called, that meant the other guy must be the police detective she'd heard him mention so often. She switched her gaze to the suited man and watched him side step between the cars in the driveway as he approached. Her mouth went dry. Jeff had talked about the tough detective, said he was one of the most thorough interrogators on the force. Looked as though she was about to see him in action—firsthand.

When the door opened, Sam exploded outward and leaped up to plant his paws on Scott's chest.

"It's okay, boy." Scott rubbed the velvety ears with

vigor and tilted his head backward to avoid a wet tongue on the mouth. "You can come out, but you've got to stay with me, okay?"

He gave the dog's neck a final brisk rub and pushed him gently away. As soon as his front paws hit the ground Sam started toward the barn, but stopped when Scott said in a low, firm voice, "This way, Sam."

He led the yellow lab to the grass beside the house and waited while Sam sniffed around the bushes to find a suitable place to relieve himself. That done, the dog tried to make another dash for the barn, but again obeyed Scott's command to "Come!" They returned together to the small knot of people standing around Becky's car and arrived in time to hear the newcomers' introduction.

The man in the suit nodded at the sheriff. "'Morning, Holmes." He then extended a hand toward Lee. "Detective Glenn Foster, with the Kentucky State Police. This is Trooper Jeff Whitley."

Lee shook both policemen's hands. "Detective, I'm Leland Courtney, owner of Shady Acres next door." He dipped his head toward the others who clustered around him. "This is Zachary Garrett, my general manager, and Scott Lewis, my assistant manager. And this is Becky Dennison, who works, ah, worked for Neal Haldeman."

The detective, a fiftyish man with a mustache, shook Garrett's hand first, then turned to Scott. He had a firm grip, the kind that made Scott want to look him straight in the eye. Scott nodded toward the uniformed trooper, who stood slightly behind Foster.

Becky shook the detective's hand. Her throat convulsed as she glanced over the detective's shoulder at Whitley. The cop gave her a reassuring smile. Scott thought he could like this guy. Not so sure about the detective. With that direct stare of his, Scott wouldn't be surprised if he whipped out a magnifying glass.

"Mrs. Dennison and I know each other," Whitley said. When Foster raised an eyebrow in his direction, Whitley lifted a shoulder. "We go to the same church."

Scott glanced at Becky with new interest. She attended church? For the first time, he noticed a glimpse of gold at her neck, almost hidden by the collar of her dirt-covered blouse. A cross. Definitely not Haldeman's type then.

Foster caught and held her gaze. "I understand you found the body?" Two bright spots of color appeared on her cheeks as she nodded. The detective turned to the trooper. "Whitley, check out the crime scene. Make sure nobody has touched anything, and keep everyone out of the way until the lab boys arrive."

Whitley nodded, and Sheriff Holmes volunteered to take him to the body. Beside Scott, Sam whimpered as he watched the two men walk toward the barn. Scott rested a hand on the dog's back.

Foster turned back to Becky. "Tell me what happened, Mrs. Dennison."

Becky began to recount her morning, but Scott's thoughts snagged for a moment on the detective's words. He called her *Mrs.* Dennison. She was married, then.

Yep, she definitely reminded him more and more of Megan.

Becky described her morning, beginning from the time she arrived at the Pasture for work. She had pathetically little to say. Why did Detective Foster's eyelids narrow? Did he suspect her of holding something back?

"That's all I know, Detective." She looked him in the eye. "As soon as I realized Neal was dead, I called 9-1-1, and then Mr. Courtney. But I got Mr. Lewis instead."

"Why did you call Mr. Courtney?"

"Because he owns this land, and he's on the Pasture's board of directors. I thought he would want to know."

He held her gaze for a long moment, then jerked a nod. Becky relaxed when the detective's focus shifted toward Mr. Courtney.

"What exactly is your relationship with the deceased?"

"I've known Haldeman for years. He used to sell equipment and supplies to breeders all over the country. Then a few years ago he approached me with an idea for a farm for retired champions. That was right after we found out about Ferdinand."

The detective's eyebrows rose. "Ferdinand?"

The older gentleman dipped his head to level a disbelieving stare at Foster through piercing blue eyes. "You don't know Ferdinand?"

Scott's head turned toward her to hide the grin twitching at his mouth. Mr. Courtney's disapproval radiated as he glared, incredulous, at Detective Foster. Becky had to bite back a grin of her own. When she applied for this job just a few months ago, she'd never heard of Ferdinand, either.

Zach spoke up. "Ferdinand was a champion, one of the finest Thoroughbreds ever bred. He won the Derby in '86 and went on to take the Breeder's Cup Classic the next year. He stood stud at Claiborne Farm for a while, then went to Japan." Zach's voice suddenly trembled and his eyes blazed. "Back in 2002 he stopped producing, and they sent him to the slaughterhouse."

Both Scott's and Mr. Courtney's faces reflected Zach's

outrage. Becky had heard Neal tell the story dozens of times with the same indignation until she'd caught a little of their righteous anger herself.

Detective Foster's expression remained impassive. He looked toward Mr. Courtney. "And then?"

The older man sighed. "The problem with stallions is they're difficult, hard to deal with. They can't paddock with other horses, so they require a lot of space. Haldeman's idea was to start Out to Pasture, one of the only retirement farms for stallions in the world. He and I worked together to set it up legally, get tax exemption status, sponsors, everything. We arranged a lease agreement for the land, set up the paddocks, and a few months later we rescued our first champion, Rusty Racer, from the same farm in Asia where Ferdinand stood."

Becky looked toward Rusty's paddock. The chestnut stallion had positioned himself in the far corner, his tail turned toward all the excitement by the house and barn as though to protest the disturbance of his peaceful day.

"So Out to Pasture leases this land from you?"

"That's right." Mr. Courtney's arm made a wide arc. "My farm, Shady Acres, is all around this place."

Foster looked first at Zach and then at Scott. "And you two work for Mr. Courtney?"

Zach nodded, and Scott said, "That's right."

Another car arrived and four men got out. The detective pursed his lips.

"Those are the lab boys from Frankfort. I need to spend some time with them, but I'll want to talk to each of you later."

His gaze slid around the small circle, coming to rest at last on Becky. She forced herself to return his look calmly, though her pulse pounded in her ears at the thought of being questioned again. She managed a nod, and he seemed satisfied.

"Interesting man," said Mr. Courtney as they watched Foster's retreating back. "Hope he's good."

Becky had heard Jeff Whitley sing the detective's praises at church often enough. "They say he's the best in the state."

"Can't say I like his attitude much," said Scott. "Seems a bit arrogant."

Mr. Courtney shrugged a shoulder. "Arrogance is permissible, as long as you have something to back it up."

Zach inclined his head toward the road. "We've got more company."

Mr. Courtney's gaze followed Zach's gesture, and his eyelids narrowed. "What's he doing here?

Nicholas Stevens's BMW pulled up and parked on the other side of the road. Becky had met him several times. He and his wife made sizable donations to the Pasture and visited frequently. Nick was a Thoroughbred breeder, though a lot younger and newer to the business than Mr. Courtney. He owned a farm up the road.

"Got half the county out here, Courtney," Nick called out as he approached, stepping high across the drying grass. "Hope nothing's wrong."

Mr. Courtney's shoulders squared. He turned a smile on his neighbor, but it looked a little pasted-on to Becky. Well, that was to be expected. They were not only neighbors, they were competitors. They both had horses running at the Keeneland race track this month. In fact, she'd heard Neal talk about the rivalry between the two men.

"Bad news, I'm afraid." Mr. Courtney grasped Nick's hand, shaking his head. "Haldeman's been killed."

Nick's smile melted. "Killed? Like an accident or something?"

"Not likely," Scott answered. "Not from the look of him."

"But…" Nick looked at each of them in turn, face pale. "But I just saw him yesterday. He was fine."

Becky felt a flash of sympathy for the man. She saw Neal yesterday, too. Seemed impossible that he could be dead now.

Mr. Courtney softened. "You might tell the detective that. He'll probably want to know what time you saw him."

Nick nodded and looked toward the barn. "I was just on my way into town for an appointment and stopped when I saw all the cars. Let me make a call to cancel."

He walked toward his BMW, shaking his head.

Behind them, Alidor gave a loud whinny. Becky whirled to find the stallion watching them. He tossed his head and issued another insistent call, but his tone didn't sound as anxious as it had this morning. He was probably hungry. In all the excitement, none of the horses had been fed.

"What are we going to do about the Pasture?" she asked Mr. Courtney. "I'll help, but I don't know anything about caring for horses."

The distinguished gentleman looked at Scott. "Feel up to taking over for a while?"

Zach's spine stiffened. "No offense to Scott, but I think I'd be a better choice." He gave Scott a brief smile of apology.

Mr. Courtney raised an eyebrow. "Why is that?"

"I have more experience with stallions." Zach's answer came instantly.

Beside Becky, Scott's jaw clenched. He obviously didn't like the insinuation that he didn't know as much as his boss, but he held his tongue.

"That's why I want you to handle things back home." Mr.

Courtney slapped Zach on the back. "I need my most experienced manager in charge during breeding season. I know I won't have to worry about a thing with you running the show."

Zach considered that compliment for a fraction of a second before he gave a single nod of acceptance. He clapped Scott on the back. "If you need a hand, son, just holler. I'll help any way I can."

"Think you can handle it?" Mr. Courtney asked Scott.

Scott straightened. "Yes, sir. I'd like that."

"Good." Mr. Courtney stepped forward to place one arm around Scott's shoulders and the other around Becky. "Zach will handle Shady Acres, and you two can manage things here. I'll call an emergency meeting of the board within the next week or so, and we'll figure out what to do from there."

Becky felt a burden settle on her shoulders along with the weight of his arm. Neal had loved this place, these horses. What would happen to the Pasture without him? Would it shut down? Could her job be in jeopardy?

She glanced sideways to study Scott's profile as his gaze swept the paddocks of Out to Pasture. The muscles in his jaw bunched, and deep lines creased his forehead. Was he worried about stepping into Neal's shoes?

A chill crept down Becky's spine. He had a right to be worried, and she should be, too.

Whoever killed Neal was still out there.

# FOUR

Becky, leaning against her car, hefted herself upright at Detective Foster's approach. Jeff strode beside him carrying a black bag. Though she'd seen him in uniform a time or two, she'd had to readjust her thinking about him today. Here, he wasn't simply Amber's boyfriend or even just a guy at church. He was all business, his face almost as closed as Detective Foster's while he went about his murder investigation.

Murder. Becky shook her head. She still couldn't believe it. Someone she knew personally had been murdered. And her boys knew him, too. She closed her eyes. How would she explain to Jamie and Tyler what happened to Mr. Neal? Was five too young to attend a funeral? She'd have to call Daddy tonight and ask his opinion.

"Mrs. Dennison," said the detective, "how are you holding up?"

Being called *Mrs.* Dennison irritated her, but whenever she insisted on *Ms.* she felt like a radical feminist. So most of the time she ignored it, like now. "Honestly? I wish I could go inside. I've got work to do." She glanced toward the back door of the farmhouse where yet another man carrying a canvas bag with the state police emblem on it entered. The door slammed behind him with a bang.

Detective Foster shook his head, and Jeff said, "It might be several days before you're allowed back inside. They've got to process everything."

"Several days?" Becky looked away so they wouldn't see the worry in her eyes. Several days without work meant several days without pay. She couldn't afford that right now, not with summer approaching. Her day care costs would double when school let out next month.

When she looked back at them, she found Foster watching her carefully. He didn't look as though he missed much. "Maybe tomorrow. The inside looks pretty clean so far. No sign of a struggle like in the barn."

Becky rubbed her hands on her arms. The sun had done its job warming the cool morning air, but she could not stop shivering. Every time she pictured Neal's body sprawled in the dirt, a chill shot down her spine.

Jeff scanned the paddocks where the horses grazed quietly. "Where's Lewis?"

"He went over to Shady Acres to check on a few things. He'll be right back."

Jeff slapped the bag against his thigh. "Look, Becky, I hate to do this but I'm going to need your shoes."

Startled, she searched his face. He returned her gaze apologetically. "My shoes? Why?"

Foster answered. "We need to match them to some prints we found in the barn."

Okay, that made sense. But she felt strange having her shoes confiscated, almost as though they thought she had something to do with the murder. Her face grew warm as she leaned against the car to lift her foot.

Jeff pulled on a blue rubber glove before taking the shoe. He immediately turned it over and showed the sole to Foster. There wasn't much tread on the bottom of her pumps, but dirt encrusted what little was there. The two men exchanged a glance.

"I've already told you I was in the barn this morning." She struggled to keep her voice even. Detective Foster would certainly notice if she acted defensively and might interpret that as guilt.

"Are you in the barn regularly?" Foster watched her closely.

Becky shook her head. "I've been in there a couple of times, like when I need to take something to Neal. Mostly I stay in the office." She shifted her weight from her bare foot to the other. Why were they staring at her like that? "That's my job. I'm an office assistant, not a farmhand."

"Were you in the barn yesterday?" asked Jeff.

Becky went over the day in her mind. They were working on the next issue of the newsletter, and she'd been focused on that most of the day. "No. The last time was on Friday."

"Do you wear other shoes to work, Mrs. Dennison?" Detective Foster's eyelids narrowed. "Ones with narrower heels, perhaps?"

Narrower heels? Becky glanced at the wide one-inch heel on the pump in Jeff's hand. "No, I don't."

The men exchanged another glance, and Foster nodded.

"Do you know of any women who might have been in the barn recently?" Jeff asked as he put her shoe into a big plastic bag.

Becky slipped her other pump off and handed it to him. They must have found prints in the barn from a narrow heel. She couldn't remember ever seeing anyone except Neal go in there. He gave tours several times a week, but the visitors came into the office to watch videos of the stallions' championship races, and then followed Neal around the paddocks, listening to each horse's life story.

Still, it wasn't impossible for one of them to step inside the barn. "I suppose someone on a tour might have." Doubt sounded in her voice.

Foster pursed his lips. "Was there a tour yesterday?"

"No. The last one was Monday."

Foster looked disappointed, and Jeff shook his head as he zipped the bag shut. The prints they found must be fresh.

Tours! The conversation sparked Becky's memory. "Speaking of tours, we have one scheduled at eleven." She glanced at her watch. "No time to call them to reschedule. They'll be here any minute."

"When they show up," said Jeff, "we'll let them know their tour's been canceled."

At that moment Scott's pickup pulled to a stop in front of the house. They watched him back carefully into the grass, avoiding the overcrowded driveway, and pull around to the rear of the house. He parked close to the edge of the driveway and opened the door. Sam followed him out, leaping from inside the cab to the ground.

Her new boss crossed the grass toward them, the dog at his side, and fixed a direct gaze on Detective Foster. "I need to get to the feed bin in the barn. The horses have to eat."

The detective frowned. "Can't you borrow some horse food from Mr. Courtney's place until we clear the scene?"

Scott looked incredulous for a moment, then his expression became patient as he explained. "Horses have extremely fragile digestive systems. A sudden change in feed can cause serious problems. Something like colic can actually put an animal down. These horses are fed a compound specially designed for older horses, and we don't keep anything like that over at Shady Acres." He cocked his head. "If I knew what brand to get, I suppose we could go buy some."

Foster and Jeff exchanged a glance. "That would probably be best."

"We have an account at Simpson's," Becky volunteered. "They'll have records on the brand and all that."

As though reminded of her presence, Scott gave her a startled look. His gaze dropped to her shoes in Jeff's plastic bag. "What's going on?"

Heat crept up her neck. She seemed to be doing a lot of blushing this morning. "They just need to compare my footprints to some they found in the barn."

Why did he have to be so handsome? Her pulse quickened as she stood under the weight of his stare. Working with the guy wouldn't be easy if she couldn't control her reactions any better than this. She drew in a deep breath and returned his gaze with a calm smile. "Do you need any help feeding the horses?"

He looked down at her nylon-clad feet, and his lips twisted into a lopsided grin. "You're going to help barefoot?"

Her cheeks blazed. "Of course not. I'll, uh, I'll go home and get some more shoes."

A knowing smile lurked behind Jeff's eyes. Amber's boyfriend had returned. Becky ignored him.

"Actually," said Foster, "you might as well stay at home. You won't be able to get into the office today, and the fewer people we have hanging around here the better. We've got your statement, and we know where to find you if we need anything else."

Escaping for home sounded like an excellent idea. She looked at Scott, her eyebrows arched in a silent request for permission. He returned her gaze for a moment, confusion creasing his brow, before his forehead cleared. Apparently, he had just realized that running the Pasture meant he was her boss.

"Oh, yeah, sure." He flashed a smile. "No sense hanging around here today. I can handle the horses. We'll start fresh tomorrow, right?"

He looked toward Jeff and Foster for verification, but Foster wasn't ready to commit. "If we're finished in there."

Becky didn't waste another minute. Time to get out of here, pay or no pay. "Okay, I'll see you in the morning." She whirled and slipped into her car. The engine turned over a couple of times before it started, but when it did the men stepped away. She backed up as far as she could, then pulled onto the grass and followed the trail through the yard and onto the road toward home.

Scott emptied a scoop of feed into Fortune's feed bucket. The horse stood a short distance away and eyed him warily.

"It's okay, fella. You'll get used to me in a day or two."

Fortune didn't appear convinced. Scott had seen the way this horse responded to Haldeman, running to the fence to be close to the man whenever he was outside. The same stallion was keeping a cautious distance from Scott, even though he was delivering food.

Or maybe it wasn't the change in servers that made Fortune distrustful; maybe it was the smaller portion. Since Scott had no idea how much Haldeman generally gave the retirees, they'd have to make do with pasture grass and a couple of scoops of the Triple Crown Senior he'd picked up at Simpson's until he could get to the records. Hopefully by tomorrow the cops would let them into the office.

He was sure Haldeman kept a file on each of the horses, their eating habits and preferences and any medications they might be on. He'd ask Becky to pull the files for him.

Becky. He poured a second scoop of feed into the bucket. He didn't know what to make of her. She looked a little flustered when she left, barefoot and covered in dirt. But throughout the morning she'd handled herself well, after the initial shock of finding Haldeman's body wore off. From her phone call, he'd have pegged her for the hysterical type, not the kind to keep her composure under police questioning. Megan would have…

He stabbed the scoop into the feed bag and climbed behind the wheel of the golf cart to head for the next paddock. Why did he keep comparing her to Megan? She didn't look a thing like his former girlfriend, except for the eyes. He steeled himself against the wave of regret that thoughts of Megan always brought. He had to stop thinking about the past and focus on the task at hand. And that meant working with Becky to hold things together. Hopefully, she was happily married and totally in love with her husband. Theirs would be a business relationship, period. And he was the boss.

A smile tugged at his mouth. He'd never officially been the boss of anyone before. This temporary job at the Pasture was going to give him some great experience. If he handled it well, he might be able to land a job as general manager with the next breeder he worked for. Having someone like Mr. Courtney put in a good word for him when he was ready to move on would be worth a lot.

He pulled on the hand brake as he approached the feed bucket for Samson's Secret. Zach's comment about having more experience with stallions than Scott wasn't really accurate. He and Mr. Courtney seemed to have forgotten that

Scott's last job had been at a stud farm. But out of respect for his boss, Scott had kept his mouth shut. Though he could be a bit crusty, Zach had been nothing but kind to Scott since his arrival. In some ways, he reminded Scott of his dad.

Unlike Fortune, Samson ran toward Scott eagerly when he realized food was being scooped into his feed bucket. He shoved his head in after the first scoop as though starving.

"Take it easy, fella." Scott laughed as he gently pushed the horse's head back so he could add another scoop. "You can't fool me into thinking you're that hungry. I've watched you graze all morning."

As he left Samson's paddock, Detective Foster and Trooper Whitley came through the back door of the farmhouse. Foster's gaze swept the paddocks and stopped when he caught sight of Scott. Both men started toward him. Scott hopped into the golf cart and met them at the edge of the black plank fencing.

"Lewis," said Foster, "any idea what this is?"

Trooper Whitley held a scrap of paper in his blue-gloved hand. When Scott reached for it, he jerked it away.

"Fingerprints," he explained.

Scott nodded and shoved his hand into his pocket. The square of paper looked like newsprint and had two ripped edges, as though torn from the corner of a larger piece. Scrawled in blue ink across the white space were two sentences.

*I need to see you. I'll come by tonight.*

The handwriting was pretty, the even, rounded letters flowing across the paper. The *i* in *tonight* was dotted with a little circle.

Scott shrugged. "I'm not an expert, but to me it looks like a note written by a woman."

Detective Foster's lips pursed. "We know that. I'm asking about the paper it's written on."

Scott looked again. The scrap was torn from the page of a racing form. Bold print beside the blue scrawl listed statistics that might look like gibberish to someone with no knowledge of the industry, but were a horse's lifetime stats.

"It's probably torn from a page of the *Daily Racing Form*." He grasped Whitley's rubber-encased wrist and turned it over. On the back the large bold heading was torn, the last part missing, but enough of the name remained that Scott recognized it. "Lemon Sugar. She's a filly from Harwood Farm over in Lexington. She ran at Keeneland this week."

Foster's face remained impassive. The man was a master at hiding his reactions. "What day?"

Scott shrugged. "I'm not sure. I don't go to the races much."

"But you're a horse guy." Whitley gave him a surprised look. "You work for a breeder."

"And you think everyone who has anything to do with Thoroughbreds is a racing enthusiast." Scott laughed. "Would you believe I've never even been to the Derby?"

"Yet you recognize the name of a horse and even know the week it's scheduled to race." Foster's statement held a question.

"Professional interest." Scott shrugged. "I might not bet on the races, but I can tell you something about the record of every horse we've bred since I came to Shady Acres, and their lineage." He nodded toward the paper. "In this case,

I know the manager over at Harwood. He was bragging about that filly last week."

Whitley flipped the note over again and studied the handwriting. "Did the victim ever go to the races?"

"Haldeman?" Scott threw back his head and laughed. "He never missed. The man loved the sport. He was as close to a fanatic as anyone I've ever known."

"So he would have been at Keeneland this week when this horse—" Foster gestured at the note "—raced?"

"I'm sure he was."

Foster nodded while Whitley took out a plastic bag and sealed the scrap of paper inside.

"What else can you tell us about the victim?" asked Foster.

Scott looked away, considering his answer. He should be honest with the police, of course, but he hated to say anything bad about a guy who could no longer defend himself. "I didn't know him well." Foster watched his face, waiting for him to continue. "We talked some. I met him last year when I came to work for Mr. Courtney, and we ran into each other around the farm fairly often. He loved the industry, everything about it. And he loved these horses." Scott nodded over Foster's shoulder, toward Samson. "He was passionate about saving them. You didn't want to get him started talking about Ferdinand or Alydar."

"Who is Alydar?" asked Whitley.

Scott waved a hand. "Another champion who died. Doesn't matter. The point is, Haldeman seemed determined to save every stallion he could. He had a list of horses he was watching, mostly in Japan, and he was relentless about raising the money to go get them the minute the Japanese were finished with them."

"Relentless?" One of Foster's eyebrows arched.

Scott shook his head. "I don't mean that negatively. Haldeman was smooth, a real talker. Remember that he was a salesman before he founded this place. He could get a donation from anyone, and if it meant he could save another stallion, he'd try."

Foster examined Scott from between narrowed eyelids. "What are you not saying, Mr. Lewis?"

Scott looked at the grass between their feet. "Well, I don't know this for a fact, but the talk around town says Haldeman had an eye for the ladies. Especially rich ones. I've heard it didn't matter how young or how old a woman was, if Haldeman thought he could get money out of her for the Pasture, she was fair game."

"I see."

Scott raised his chin and looked the detective in the eye. "That's really just farm talk. I don't have any personal knowledge to base it on. Haldeman and I didn't run in the same circles."

"And what circles would those be?" asked Whitley.

Scott shifted his gaze to the younger man. "I have no idea who Haldeman ran with. I'm active in my church, and that's where I spend most of my free time."

Both men nodded, and Detective Foster looked toward the farmhouse. "I think we're going to finish up in there this afternoon. You and Mrs. Dennison should be able to get back to work tomorrow."

A man came out of the barn and gestured to Foster. He tossed his head in answer. "If you think of anything else that might be helpful, you'll give us a call?" He didn't wait for a response, but headed toward the barn.

Whitley fished a card case out of his black bag and slipped a business card out of it. Scott took it, saw that it had contact information for Trooper Jeffrey Whitley, and shoved it in his jeans pocket. He glanced at the trooper. "So you go to church with Becky and her husband?"

Whitley shook his head. "Just Becky. Her husband took off when her twins were babies, I guess. She was already divorced when I met her a year ago."

Divorced. So she wasn't happily married after all. But she had kids. "Twins?"

Whitley laughed. "Five-year-old boys, and they keep her hopping. You never met a rowdier pair."

Well, that settled that. Divorced or not, Becky Dennison just dropped off his radar screen. He had no desire to get involved with the single mother of two lively mischief makers.

# FIVE

"Hi, Daddy," Becky said into the phone later that night.

"Hey, sweetheart, how's my best girl?"

She smiled at his light tone. He always sounded happy to hear from her. "I'm all right."

"Just all right?" Now he sounded concerned. "Is something wrong with the boys?"

"No, they're fine. I just put them to bed." She propped her slippered feet on the coffee table, something she insisted Jamie and Tyler never do. But the recliner had a Hot Wheels car stuck in the mechanism, and she hadn't found the time to pry it out yet.

"Out with it, then. What's bothering you?"

"Something terrible happened at work. My boss was killed, probably murdered, and I found his body this morning."

"Becky!" Alarm exploded in his voice. "Are you okay? Do I need to come out there?"

A tender smile curved her lips. Always her stalwart, if long-distance, protector, especially in the four years since Mom died. "I'm fine, Daddy, and of course you don't need to come. I just need your advice about the boys. They knew Neal, so I have to tell them something, but I'm not sure how to go about it. Do you think they're too young to go to a funeral?"

"Yes, I do." Not a hint of doubt in his voice. "But they're not too young to talk about death."

"You don't think it will affect them?"

"Sure, it will affect them. But maybe not as much as you think. They probably already know more about death than you realize. They've seen dead bugs and animals on the side of the road. And on television, no doubt."

He was right about that. She tried to monitor their television viewing, but even the cartoons were full of violence these days.

"I wouldn't tell them the man was murdered," Daddy advised. "Just say he died, and he's living in heaven now with Jesus."

Sadness gripped Becky as she realized that probably wasn't true. "I don't think Neal was a Christian. Any time I tried to discuss God or church he changed the subject."

"Well, then just tell the boys he died and leave it at that."

"Okay." She reached for her mug of herbal tea and inhaled the soothing odor of chamomile before she took a sip. "How are you doing? Everything go all right in that meeting you were worried about?"

Daddy worked for a software firm in Silicon Valley managing a staff of developers. She had only a vague idea of what they did. Sometimes when he described the details of his job she felt as if he was speaking another language.

"Smooth as silk. I talked them out of a big chunk of next year's budget to fund a new database platform in conjunction with the operating system switchover."

Like that. But she knew better than to ask him to explain what a database platform was and why it would cost a chunk of money. She'd be on the phone all night. "Good for you."

"Listen, are you sure you're okay? If this guy was murdered, are you in any danger?"

That thought had plagued Becky throughout the day. "I don't think so. It looked like there was a fight. Scott thinks maybe he surprised a burglar in the barn."

"The barn? What would a thief want from a barn? And who is Scott?"

"Scott is my new boss." Unease trickled into Becky's thoughts, but she made sure it didn't seep into her voice. "And I don't know what a thief would want. Horse equipment maybe. Some of that stuff is expensive. Or maybe it was teenagers looking for drugs. Whoever it was, the police will catch them soon. Don't worry about me."

His voice softened. "Worrying about you and my rascally grandsons is what I do best. I still wish you'd move out here so I could give you a hand with them."

Becky sipped her tea before answering. The thought of living near Daddy was attractive. But the cost of living was so high out in California there was no way she could find a job that paid well enough to support her and the boys. And she refused to move in with her father. No, she was better off staying here where at least she could be somewhat self-sufficient.

"It would be wonderful to see you more often," she admitted, as she always did, "but I'm not moving to California."

"Well, then." His voice trailed off. The faint sound of a keyboard tapping interrupted the silence. As usual, he was working on something as they talked. "Do you need any money?"

She smiled. "No, Daddy. But thanks for asking."

"You get any more checks?"

"I got one last week, in fact."

After their divorce, Christopher paid a total of three child support payments before disappearing. But four months ago, out of the blue, she started getting checks from the division of child support. When she called, all she could find out was that he'd taken a new job and his employer filed his social security number with something called the national new hire reporting database. They'd begun garnisheeing his wages. Becky didn't expect it to last, but it had been a huge relief to have extra money to put toward some of her frighteningly large credit card balances.

"If you need money, you'll let me know, right?"

How lucky she was to have such a supportive father. Even though he was on the other side of the country, she knew her boys would never go without the basic needs. She could count on him. And she'd never abuse the privilege. "I love you, Daddy."

"I love you, too, sweetheart. Don't forget to say your prayers."

# SIX

Scott snapped the lid back on the feed bin, straightened and listened to the sound of rain pelting the barn's roof. He breathed a deep breath of damp morning air. Both the front and rear doors stood open in an effort to clear out the lingering odor of death that was probably only his imagination.

He'd swept up the loose dirt beneath the place where Haldeman had lain and covered it with straw. But Sam kept leaving the rug that served as his daytime bed to circle the area, nose to the ground.

A car pulled into the driveway. Becky's Chevy. His watch showed a few minutes before eight o'clock. The engine cut off, the driver's door opened a crack and a blue umbrella popped open above the roof. Becky emerged, the slick canopy only partially shielding her from the driving rain as she made a dash toward the barn. When she stepped beneath the shelter, Sam leaped off his rug and ran to greet her.

She stopped just inside and bent down to rub the dog's head. "Hello, Sam." Her gaze went to the place where Haldeman's body had lain until the coroner took it to the morgue yesterday afternoon. She looked up at Scott. "I see the police are gone. I hoped they would be."

Scott nodded. "They finished up sometime after

midnight. They're coming back this afternoon, though. They want to get your fingerprints."

Eyes wide, her hand flew to her chest. "Mine? Why?"

"It's nothing to worry about," he assured her. "They found a bunch of prints in the office and out here. They just need to be able to eliminate yours."

A vertical crease appeared between her eyebrows. "What if I don't want them to have my fingerprints?"

Actually, Scott asked that same question when they came for his. Until yesterday he hadn't been at the Pasture in months, and he didn't see the need. But Foster said since he was present at the scene of a crime when law enforcement arrived, they needed his, too. It felt kind of creepy having your fingerprints on file with the state police. "They said they'd call the county attorney and get a warrant if necessary."

"Oh."

She looked nice today in dress slacks and a pink sweater. He glanced at her shoes. Women's shoes, not sneakers or boots. Obviously not farm attire.

"You don't help with the horses much, do you?"

Her eyes went wide. "Neal never asked me to. I handle pretty much everything in the office. He even turned over the bank account a few weeks ago, so I make the deposits and write checks and all that." She swallowed convulsively. "Do you need help out here?"

Scott studied her. She looked frightened. "Are you afraid of horses?"

"A little," she admitted. "I've never been around them much. They're so…so big."

Scott laughed. "They're big, all right. And some of them can be temperamental, especially stallions. But they're also smart and love to have fun. They each have their own personality and quirks, just like people." He nodded toward the paddocks behind the barn. "You should get to know them, maybe help me take care of them. A lot of people would jump at the chance. We've got some real celebrities here."

Doubt clouded her features, but she said, "I'm sure you're right." Suddenly her face cleared. "Before I forget to tell you, a volunteer group from the university will be here after lunch to help groom them. They come every Friday afternoon."

That made sense. The university boasted an equine research center as part of its veterinary medicine program. Scott had instructed student volunteers over at Shady Acres more times than he could count.

He glanced through the doorway at the dark, heavy sky. "I hope it clears up." The clouds looked as though they had settled in for a while. He looked back down at Becky. "Would you do me a favor?"

"Of course."

"I'm sure Haldeman kept files on each of these horses, with vet records and the like. I want to take a look at them. And if you can find anything else that might help me figure out how things work around here, I'd appreciate it. Oh, and Detective Foster said if you run across anything in the office that might help with their investigation, you're supposed to call Trooper Whitley. I put his card on the desk inside."

Becky glanced toward the house. "Are you going to live in there, like Neal did?"

Scott had considered the question several times yesterday. Though it wasn't a bad idea to have someone on-site at night, the thought of moving into Haldeman's bedroom was not an appealing one. Scott rented a cottage from Mr.

Courtney on the far side of Shady Acres, and he'd come to the conclusion that it was close enough. "I don't think so. Sam and I did okay last night. Oh, yeah." He snapped his fingers as he remembered a detail the dog certainly had not forgotten. "Could you feed Sam? I didn't have anything to give him over at my place."

Becky's smile made her eyes shine even in the gloom inside the barn. She was a pretty woman. Sweet and whole-some-looking. When she spoke, affection for the dog warmed her tone. "I always feed Sam when I get to work, while Neal's out feeding the horses." She bent again and roughed the yellow fur on the dog's neck. "Come on, boy. Let's go get you some breakfast."

She nodded in Scott's direction as she popped her umbrella open. With a quick glance at the menacing sky, she dashed out of the barn and splashed across the wet driveway toward the house, Sam running ahead of her.

Scott watched until the door closed behind them. What was he thinking, encouraging her to get involved with the horses? If she helped care for them, he'd be forced to spend more time with her.

Maybe she'd forget his suggestion. Better for everyone if she stayed in the office and let him handle the horses.


Seated in front of Neal's two-drawer file cabinet, Becky looked up when the back door opened. Scott stopped just inside the next room to wipe his feet on a tattered but still-serviceable floor mat. Sam leaped off a shabby recliner where he'd been napping and went to greet his new master.

At least, she assumed Scott had decided to adopt the dog. Becky had been half-ready to suggest that Sam could come home with her. The boys would love to welcome him to the family, and he could still come to work with her every day. But he seemed to like Scott, and she couldn't afford to feed an extra mouth anyway.

From the office, which had once been the living room of the old farmhouse, Becky called to him. "I found the files you asked me to pull."

Scott appeared in the doorway between the two rooms. He leaned a shoulder against the frame.

"Thanks. Do you know where Haldeman kept treats for the horses? There aren't any in the barns."

"Sure, they're in here."

He didn't move as she slid past him in the doorway. The scent of horses clung to him, an earthy, pleasant odor that reminded her of the outdoors. She looked up into his solemn face. He was a lot less jovial than Neal, who had always liked to make wisecracks. And a lot more handsome.

She led him into the kitchen. "Their favorites are carrots and apples. Neal did live here, of course, so there's some food that will need to be disposed of."

She opened the refrigerator and showed him the nearly empty interior. On the shelves were several take-out containers which had probably been there for weeks, a bag of apples and an unopened half-gallon of milk. "He wasn't much of a cook."

Scott peered inside. "If that milk's any good, you might as well take it home. Your boys will drink it, no doubt."

Becky turned a quick look on him. How did he know about Jamie and Tyler? Had she mentioned them yesterday? No, she didn't think so. Her pulse quickened as she looked into his dark eyes. Did he ask around about her?

She tore her gaze away and closed the refrigerator. "Thanks. I'll do that. We keep treats for the horses here."

She opened one of the cabinets. Inside were a dozen or so bags of peppermint-flavored horse treats. "They prefer carrots, but—"

From the other room came the sound of the back door slamming. "Hello? Is anyone here?"

A woman stepped into view. She was model-thin and tall, nearly as tall as Scott. Her artful makeup, tailored skirt, boots and elegant suede jacket with fur trim looked out of place in the dumpy little farmhouse-turned-office. When she caught sight of them, she came into the kitchen. The odor of her sweet, musky perfume filled the room.

She stopped just inside, her gaze sweeping over Becky, who fiddled with the cross that hung from her neck. Suddenly she felt short and dumpy in her slacks and sweater. Superiority flickered in the woman's eyes as her chin rose a fraction, and she turned her attention on Scott, dismissing Becky with a flip of shining blond hair.

Her carefully shaped eyebrows rose as she gave Scott the same once-over. "My, my, my. And who do we have here?"

Becky almost laughed out loud. Nobody pronounced it 'he-yah' like that on purpose. That deep Southern drawl had to be fake, as fake as her tan. Who had a tan like that in April, anyway?

Scott crossed the room in two steps, his hand extended. "Scott Lewis. I'm taking care of things here at Out to Pasture for a little while."

The woman's movement was smooth, silky, as she took Scott's hand. Her other arm rose to cover their clasped hands, and her long fingers brushed slowly over Scott's skin. "I am Kaci Buchanan." She tilted her head and peered at Scott from the corners of her eyes. "Have we met, Mr. Lewis? Perhaps at the Thoroughbred Club?"

Becky had to stop herself from rolling her eyes. Judging by the number of syllables the woman got out of each word, she must love hearing her own voice. Every sentence was its own little production. Nobody would fall for that assumed accent.

Scott shook his head. "I don't think so. I'm not a member of the Thoroughbred Club. And I'm sure I'd remember if we met somewhere else."

"You simply *must* become a member, darling. *Everyone* is, you know." Still clutching his hand, she leaned forward until her face was inches from his. "I'd be honored to sponsor you, given your new position."

A smile broke on Scott's face. "Thank you, Miss Buchanan. That's very nice of you."

"Please call me Kaci. Everyone does."

They appeared to have completely forgotten about Becky. She pasted on a pleasant smile and took a step forward. "What can we do for you, Kaci? I'm afraid we don't have any tours scheduled this morning."

Arrogance flooded her delicate features as Kaci tore her gaze away from Scott. Apparently, the invitation to use her first name was not extended to Becky. At least she released Scott's hand, and with a quick glance in Becky's direction, he shoved it in the back pocket of his jeans.

"Why, aren't you the sweetest thing." Her chilly tone contradicted her words. "But I've not come for a tour. Neal gave me one personally." Her gaze slid back to Scott and a smile flirted with her lips as her tone warmed. "After hours."

Amazing. She managed to flirt with one guy at the same time she hinted at an intimate relationship with another. Pink spots appeared on Scott's ruddy cheeks. Becky bit back a grunt of disgust. Surely he wasn't taken in by this, this fake Southern belle.

He cleared his throat. "I suppose you've heard about Haldeman?"

Kaci's face became mournful. "Simply dreadful. And such a shock." She lifted a graceful hand to rest at the base of her throat. "Neal and I had a *special* relationship, you know. When I read the news of his demise in the morning paper…" An elegant and perfectly manicured hand fluttered dramatically around her collarbone.

Becky didn't believe her for a minute. She knew Neal dated frequently, and sitting in the same office during the day she couldn't help but overhear the occasional phone conversation. She had heard him mention the name Kaci, had passed along an occasional message from her for Neal to return her call. But she'd taken messages from many women.

Kaci apparently recovered enough to continue. "I came by to pay my respects to dear Neal."

Becky folded her arms across her chest. "So you won't be coming to the funeral?"

Kaci's smile stiffened, her gaze shifting to Becky. "This is the place he loved. I shall always remember him here, as he was the last time I saw him."

Scott nodded, his face full of sympathy, which made Becky's fingers dig into her arms. Puh-lease! "You're welcome to walk around the farm, see the horses again if you like."

She gave a short laugh and gestured toward her fancy leather boots. "Not dressed like this, darling. No, I'm heading to the track right now, where I can shelter from the weather in Mother's box." She half turned toward the door, and then stopped. "While I'm thinking of it, I left an item here not long ago. A personal item. I'd like to have it back."

Aha. Becky studied her through narrowed eyelids. The real reason for this visit had emerged. "And what might that be?"

"An earring." She shot a coy glance toward Scott. "I know just where it is. If you don't mind?"

Without waiting for permission she turned and went through the doorway toward the television room.

Becky speared Scott with an open-eyed glance. "Stop her," she hissed.

He held out his hands, confused. "Why? If she left something here, she has every right to get it back."

Becky gave him an incredulous look as she brushed past him on the way down the hallway. "The police might like to know about whatever it is."

He followed her, and found Kaci bending gracefully over the sagging sofa, her hand shoved into the crack behind the cushion.

"There it is." She straightened and rose in a smooth motion, her hand held out for their inspection. Resting in her palm was a large diamond earring. The way the stone sparkled in the room's dull light told Becky it was not an imitation.

"I can see why you'd want to get that back." Scott spoke to Kaci, but leveled a triumphant look on Becky.

"They were a gift. When I got home from my last visit and realized I was only wearing one, I knew it must have fallen out." Kaci practically purred as she gazed at the diamond. Then she closed her fingers around it. "I'd best run along. You will consider the Club, now, won't you, darling?"

She flounced out of the room. Scott grinned at Becky and lifted a shoulder before following. His amused expression soothed her feathers a little. Maybe he hadn't been taken in by the flirty floozie after all. Becky stood inside, watching through the window as he gallantly opened the car door. With a new wave of disgust she noticed that Kaci drove a gorgeous BMW convertible.

Kaci fluttered her fingers at Scott as she backed out of the driveway. Becky didn't wait for him to come back inside, but went into the office. He arrived as she lifted the remaining file folders out of the cabinet and deposited them with the others on Neal's desk.

"You didn't like her very much."

His dry tone made her turn a sharp look his way. A denial rose to her lips, but she bit it back. No sense lying. "I'm not crazy about fakes in any form."

His brows drew together. "Fakes? Do you know who that was? Kaci Buchanan is the daughter of Francine Buchanan, one of the richest and most influential horse breeders in the industry. She's not a fake. Kaci's the real deal."

"Oh, I don't mean the money." Becky twisted her lips. "You can't fake that. I mean her—the accent, the attitude. And especially her excuse for coming here." Becky thrust her chin in the air and imitated the Southern drawl. "Oh, darling, I want to remember dear Neal in the place he loved." She blew a raspberry. "Not likely. She was here to get that earring before the police found it and started asking questions about its owner."

Scott threw back his head and laughed. "Are you sure you're not the tiniest bit jealous?"

Becky drew herself up, outraged. "Jealous of what? Her money?"

She turned her back on him and reached down to straighten the pile of folders. Jealous? Of a society brat? Not a chance.

But when she remembered Kaci's arrogance as her gaze swept over her, her face heated with remembered shame. Kaci had probably never bought a pair of pants at Wal-Mart in her life. She probably didn't even have to pay for her own clothes, or her car, or anything. She definitely had never searched the couch cushions for change to buy gasoline.

And the way she flirted so blatantly. Even worse, Scott seemed to actually enjoy the attention, in a detached, amused sort of way.

Jealous? Okay, maybe a little.

She faced Scott. "I'm prepared to concede that I might have felt a touch of jealousy. But you have to admit, her whole attitude was strange."

"How so?"

"If she and Neal had a 'special relationship,' she sure didn't seem very upset by his death, did she?"

He considered that, then shook his head. "She didn't seem grief-stricken."

"As I said, she came here today for one reason only. To get that earring."

Scott's forehead dipped forward. "Granted. But you can't blame her for wanting it back. That diamond had to be worth a small fortune. She must have been frantic to recover it."

Becky wasn't buying that. "First of all, she doesn't look like the kind who'd be worried over the cost of an earring, no matter what it's worth. No, either she has some reason for not wanting the police to know she's been here recently, or she left that earring here on purpose."

"You mean so she had an excuse to come back and see Haldeman again."

Becky relaxed. At least he wasn't too trusting to spot

manipulative behavior. "Exactly. She went straight to it, which can only mean she planted it there."

Scott chuckled, shaking his head. "She's a conniving female, I'll give you that. But she wouldn't be the first to pull that stunt. There's nothing of any possible interest to the police."

"Maybe." Becky shoved the top drawer on the file cabinet closed and crossed the room to her desk. "But did you see her shoes?"

"Boots," he corrected. "And what about them?"

She slid into her chair, picked up a piece of mail and caught his gaze across the room. "They had high, narrow heels."

# SEVEN

Scott had already started grooming Dark Diego when the students from the university showed up. The dark clouds had emptied themselves out midmorning, and the sun shining overhead had dried the horses enough that they could be groomed. His helpers, three girls and a guy, already knew about Haldeman's death when they arrived.

"I just can't believe it."

Scott lifted his head to look toward the place where the four were perched on the fence, arms dangling over the top plank, while he ran the currycomb gently over Diego's back.

The pretty brunette, who introduced herself as Patti, shook her head. "I mean, last week he was totally fine."

The boy beside her, Mike, gave her a sideways glance. "He was killed. It's not like you'd be able to see it coming last Friday." He turned toward Scott. "And you saw the body?"

His expression begged for details, but Scott refused to feed the kid's morbid curiosity. He ran the comb over the stallion's flank. "Yeah."

"So, was there, like, blood and gore?"

"Mike, you're disgusting." Rachel looked at Scott. "I'm going to miss Mr. Haldeman. He really loved these horses."

"I know he did." Scott gave the chestnut's hair a final

swipe with the currycomb. "Could you hand me the dandy brush, please?" He pointed toward the pouch hanging on a fence post.

Patti dug out the brush and passed it over the fence. Scott stepped back up to Diego's head and started at the top of his neck. As he flicked the brush expertly, Diego's eyelids half closed, and his lower lip quivered with pleasure.

"He likes this," Scott said.

The third girl, Teri, agreed. "Yeah, Diego loves it. Not like Alidor over there."

Scott glanced at the next paddock where Alidor grazed near his run-in shack. "A bit feisty, is he?"

All four nodded. "Mr. Haldeman didn't let us mess with him much," said Mike. "Not unless Alidor was in a real good mood."

"But we can groom the others," said Patti. "Do you want us to get started?"

Scott looked at their eager faces. Actually, he preferred to groom all the stallions himself, at least this first time. That way they'd have an opportunity to get used to him, and he'd be able to do a quick checkup on each of them. On the other hand, if the horses were accustomed to having these four around they might appreciate seeing someone familiar in Haldeman's absence.

"Sure, go ahead. I'll come around and give you a hand so I can check each one out."

With a nod they hopped off the fence and headed toward the barn. Their voices faded as they rounded the corner and disappeared inside. Scott went over Diego with the dandy brush and then swapped it for a body brush. The stallion stood with his ears perked forward, obviously enjoying himself.

He'd read Diego's file this morning. The stallion was something of a legend in the Florida racing circuit, having fathered more than five hundred stakes winners. An impressive record, and by far the most successful in terms of his career as a stud, though his lifetime earnings as a racer didn't come close to that of some of the horses at the Pasture.

Scott laughed at the horse's delight as the soft-bristled brush caressed his forelock. "Yeah, this is the life, isn't it? You've got a big space to run, tender spring grass, an automatic waterer, someone to bring your food every morning and night, and you get groomed every week to boot." He ran the brush over the horse's face with a slow, careful motion. "That's what retirement is all about, huh, boy?"

As Diego's ears flicked forward, Scott caught sight of a spot on his left ear. He lowered the brush and reached up with his other hand to touch an irregular place along the edge. Diego tossed his head away when Scott's fingers touched it. There was a nick along the edge, healed up but not scarred over.

"What'd you do to yourself, Diego? Get in a fight?"

No telling how old the cut was, but it wasn't fresh. The stallion probably cut it rubbing his head against the ground or something. Judging by the amount of dirt caked under his hair, Diego enjoyed a good roll.

"Hey, Mr. Lewis."

Scott looked up to see Mike coming out of the barn, grooming tools in his hands. The girls followed, and two of them peeled off to head in the direction of Gadsby's paddock. Rachel followed Mike toward him.

"Any idea where the other hoof pick went?"

Scott nodded toward the bag hanging on the fence post.

"There's one in there. Just let me finish up with Diego here and you can have it."

A polishing rag in her hand, Rachel shook her head. "No, he means the other one. There should be three, but one seems to be missing."

Scott's hand stopped halfway through a brush swipe. The fine hair at the base of his scalp prickled. Foster said he should be sure to let him know if anything came up missing. Of course, Scott wouldn't have any idea what might be missing from the Pasture's barn, because he didn't spend any time there. But these kids did.

He pulled the bag off the fence post and dumped the contents onto the ground. One hoof pick. He grabbed it and held it up.

"Is this the one you're looking for?"

Mike shrugged. "It'll do as well as any of them. But Rachel's right. Mr. Haldeman kept three sets of grooming tools on that workbench in the barn, and—" The young man gasped as he realized the implication of the missing tool. "Do you think somebody used a hoof pick to kill Mr. Haldeman?"

Staring with horror at the pick in Scott's hand, Rachel looked a little green around the gills. Scott turned the tool over and examined the business end. The metal point was sharp, but not razor sharp. It wouldn't be easy to kill a man with this.

An image of Haldeman's body rose unbidden in Scott's mind. Those gashes on his chest had been ragged and wide. Ugly. Not clean punctures or slashes that a sharp knife would make. And his neck had been covered in blood. So much blood. Scott hadn't seen details, hadn't wanted to see details, but it was possible a hoof pick could gouge a man's throat.

The hand holding the hoof pick trembled. Rachel gave

a strangled cry and turned away, while Mike's eyes were round as doughnuts.

"I think I'd better call the police," Scott said.

Becky finished totaling up the bank deposit and double-checked her numbers. Two days' worth of correspondence opened and dealt with, finally. It had taken her most of the morning. The phone wouldn't stop ringing, people calling to offer their condolences after reading the article in the *Lexington Herald-Leader.* Finally, she'd recorded a generic message and let the machine pick up the calls.

The mail had yielded a few small donations from individuals, as usual, and one five-hundred-dollar check from a man who'd taken the tour three weeks ago. Neal would be pleased with—

Becky's hand froze in the act of setting down the pen. She closed her eyes and let the fact of Neal's death sweep over her again. Hard to believe he wouldn't be coming through the door any minute, whistling in that tuneless way of his as he crossed toward the kitchen to get his afternoon cup of coffee. Though Becky didn't drink coffee herself, she'd made a fresh pot at lunchtime. Habit. Maybe Scott would want a cup.

Through the back door she saw a police car pull into view and park beside Scott's pickup. They'd finally come to get her fingerprints. She pressed her lips tight. She intended to tell those people what she thought about them leaving fingerprint powder all over the office for her to clean up. And no matter what Scott thought, she'd tell them about Kaci Buchanan's visit this morning, too.

Jeff got out from behind the wheel, and Detective Foster stood on the opposite side of the car. But instead of coming into the office they walked toward the barn. She slipped the deposit into the desk drawer and then crossed the room to look out the window. Scott and all four university students came out of the barn and stood talking to them. The kids looked excited about something.

Curiosity drove her through the door. She approached the group in time to hear Rachel say, "There are *always* three hoof picks. We do three horses at a time."

Foster glanced at Jeff, who opened his leather notebook and slipped the pen from beneath the metal clip. "Can you describe the missing tool?"

"Yeah," said Mike. "It looks just like the other two. Hold on a sec." The kid dashed into the barn and returned in a moment with a tool in his hand. "Exactly like this one."

A tool missing? Becky looked at the instrument in Mike's hand. A red plastic looped handle held a curved shaft of metal that tapered to a point. Was something like this used to kill Neal? It didn't look all that sharp, but somehow that made it an even more wicked-looking weapon.

Foster took the hoof pick from Mike and turned it over in his hand. He spoke Becky's thoughts. "It isn't very sharp."

He and Jeff exchanged a glance. Watching them, Becky realized the two had expected a dull instrument like this one. Her throat constricted, trying not to think about the damage that point could inflict.

"When was the last time you saw all three hoof picks?" Jeff's glance swept the four kids.

"Friday," said Teri without hesitation, and the others nodded. "Our group comes every Friday afternoon."

"Six of us," put in Patti. "Because there are three sets of grooming tools. Last week Kelly and Josh came, but they couldn't come today."

Jeff looked at Scott. "Could it be misplaced?"

Scott shook his head. "We combed that barn after we called you. They're not sure if a polishing rag is missing or not, but they all insist the tools are kept on the workbench."

"It was there last week." Mike's expression became stubborn. "We used all three, and we always clean them and put them back. And they're always there the next Friday."

Becky remembered something Neal said earlier in the week, something about…

"Bull!"

They all looked at her. Foster's eyebrows arched. "I beg your pardon?"

She gave an embarrassed laugh. "Bulldozer Buckaroo. He's one of the stallions, and Neal sometimes grooms him during the week. I think he did this week, on Tuesday. He came into the office at lunchtime talking about…" She closed her eyes, trying to remember Neal's exact words. "He said Bull had been rolling in the mud again. He said he thought Bull did it on purpose, because he liked being groomed."

"So you think he used the hoof pick on Tuesday and didn't put it back?" Patti asked.

"I suppose it's possible."

"Not likely." Mike's eyebrows drew together. "Why would he put all the brushes back where they belong but put the hoof pick somewhere else? That doesn't make sense."

Becky agreed. Neal wasn't exactly the most organized man she'd ever known, but it didn't seem likely he'd put all but one of the tools back in place.

Scott rubbed his chin with a finger, his expression pensive. "Maybe it got broken, or maybe he dropped it on the way to or from Bull's paddock."

Mike seemed determined to prove the hoof pick as the

murder weapon. "Then he would have bought another one." He swung toward Becky. "Did he?"

"No." She spoke with confidence. "He would have asked me to do that, and he didn't."

The detective nodded slowly, then held Scott's gaze. "You'll look around for it? Let us know if you find anything?" Scott nodded. "In the meantime, may we have this one? I'd like to show it to the coroner."

Scott lifted a shoulder. "Of course." He switched his gaze to Mike. "Could you run over to Shady Acres and ask Mr. Garrett if we can borrow a couple of hoof picks for the afternoon?" Mike nodded. "And Becky, do you think you could pick up a couple of replacements?"

"Sure." She'd stop by the tack and feed store when she made the bank deposit.

Jeff slid his pen beneath the clip and snapped his notebook closed. He looked at her. "We need to get some prints from you."

His expression held a hint of apprehension, as though he was afraid she'd put up a fuss. Truthfully, Becky had considered it after the mess they'd left in the office. But if having her fingerprints helped them catch Neal's killer, she wasn't going to argue about it. "Okay, let's get it over with."

They headed toward the house and Scott fell in beside them. The girls returned to the barn, whispering together, and Mike headed toward the road and Shady Acres.

Scott spoke in a low voice as they walked. "You know, if that hoof pick was the weapon that killed Haldeman, it supports my theory that he surprised a burglar. The grooming tools are kept right out in the open on top of that workbench. Either of them could have grabbed it during a fight."

Jeff kept his eyes ahead as he opened the door for Becky

to enter. Foster smoothed down the edge of his mustache with a finger and answered noncommittally. "That's one theory we're considering."

In other words, the police weren't going to discuss their investigation. Well, that was to be expected. Becky eyed Jeff as she stepped through the doorway. Would he discuss the case with Amber? Probably not. It would be unprofessional. But just because they were being tight-lipped didn't mean she should. While Jeff took her fingerprints, she intended to tell him about Kaci's visit.

# EIGHT

"I'll see to it, Darrell. Don't worry about a thing."

Becky replaced the telephone receiver. Darrell Haldeman, Neal's only living relative as far as she knew, had been notified of his uncle's death by the state police. He'd called from his home in Texas to tell her he was making arrangements to fly to Kentucky the week after next. Instead of a funeral he'd decided on a memorial service to be held while he was in town. Becky would help with the arrangements on this end.

She eyed Neal's desk. Making service arrangements was one thing. Going through Neal's personal belongings was a different story entirely. She'd shut the door to Neal's bedroom and bathroom, and as far as she was concerned it would stay shut until Darrell Haldeman arrived.

But the desk was another matter. Its drawers held information about the Pasture, and therefore she needed to go through it to see if there was anything that might help Scott in his role of temporary manager.

Might as well tackle the biggest mess first. She sat in Neal's desk chair and slid open the deep drawer on the right. She'd seen Neal toss papers unceremoniously in there, with no thought of maintaining any sort of order. "It's my To Be Filed drawer," he'd told her with a grin.

"I'll be happy to organize it for you," she had offered.

But he'd declined. "Nah, I've got personal papers mixed in with the business stuff. Nothing important, though. All the horses' records are in their file folders."

If only Neal had been as organized with his personal records as he had been with the retirees' folders she'd given to Scott this morning. She peered into the drawer. "What a mess."

She pulled out the contents and piled them on the surface of the desk.

Two hours later, Scott stepped into the office. "What's all this?"

Kneeling on the floor, Becky looked up. "A bunch of junk, mostly, from Neal's desk. I started out trying to make a folder for everything, but there's such a mishmash of stuff here I decided it would be easier to try to sort it into broader categories." She gestured to the eight piles of papers, receipts and clippings spread over the floor.

Scott dropped onto the only seat in the office besides the desk chairs, a dilapidated old wing chair donated by someone years ago. Becky avoided it, because it smelled like a musty attic.

"What did he have in there?"

"Everything." Becky picked up the nearest pile. "There are hundreds of newspaper clippings. It's like he saved every article he ever read that had anything to do with horses or racing." She lifted the top one and held it up. "Here's one about Japanese races earning graded status, whatever that means. There's one on stud farms in Turkey and a bunch about individual horses. There's even an article in here about horse cloning." She put the clipping back with the others and reached for the next pile. "And there are dozens of letters from people who've been on the tour and wrote to thank him." She shook her head. "Why would he keep those? Some of them are two years old."

"No idea." Scott bent over and picked up a handful of register receipts from the pile nearest him. "Shouldn't these be in a financial file somewhere?"

"No, he was very good about filing financial records for the Pasture. Those are personal receipts, as far as I can tell."

Scott read from the top one. "Two pair of jeans and a men's shirt from Wal-Mart." He shuffled through the next few. "Shoes, groceries." With a shrug, he put them back on the pile.

"Here's something interesting, though I have no idea what it is." She crawled forward on her knees to reach the pile nearest the desk. "There are more than fifty notes in Neal's handwriting that look like this."

She picked up the top one, a paper torn from a spiral notebook, a couple of ragged ribbons waving from the edge as she held it up for Scott's inspection. Written on it were rows of numbers that made no sense at all.

Scott took it from her. "2.5—#5w—BC3—8-1 Pd 20." He read the numbers and letters on the first line slowly, then his gaze rose to catch hers. "This is the record for a bet. See here, up at the top, the date is November 4. That's the day the Breeder's Cup ran last year, so I'm guessing BC3 means the third race. The five is the number five horse in that race, the W means he bet it to win, and it went off at eight to one." He studied it a moment longer. "Two point five must stand for two hundred fifty dollars, and this says the horse won, so it paid two thousand dollars."

Becky gasped. "Two thousand dollars? On one race?"

Oh, what she could do with an extra two thousand dollars. There were a bunch of rows on that sheet in Scott's hand. Neal must have bet on dozens of horses.

"He got lucky on that one." Scott's eyes moved as he scanned the sheet. "Looks like he didn't come out a winner at the end of the day, though. He was out close to eight thousand dollars."

"Eight thousand?" So much for winning two thousand in one race. Becky's head swam at the thought of losing eight thousand dollars in a single day. She knew Neal liked to bet, because she overheard him talking on the phone quite a bit. But that was a lot of money! "Are you sure that's what those numbers mean, Scott?"

Scott shook his head slowly. "Not entirely. Every bettor has his own way of keeping tabs on his bets. We could check the track statistics for that day to be sure, maybe pull the racing forms over at the Keeneland Library."

"Oh!" Becky turned and picked up a pile of newspapers. The title on all of them was *Daily Racing Form.* "There were a bunch of these in the drawer, too."

Scott took the pile and rifled through them. "Here it is." He fanned the edges and flipped the paper open. "Yeah, here's the fifth horse. There's a note jotted on there, '2.5—30-1.'" He looked up at her. "That's got to be his bet and the horse's odds at post time. And this—" he held up the page from the notebook "—is his tally sheet."

Becky looked at the huge stack of papers with similar figures on them. She shook her head sadly. "Poor Neal. He must have had a real problem with gambling. I had no idea."

Scott put the racing form down and studied the figures scrawled on the paper, lines creasing his forehead. "I'll tell you what worries me is this last number on here. Looks like he added up his winnings and losses for the day and ended up in the hole eight thousand three hundred fifty dollars. But look below that."

Becky took the paper from his hand. At the bottom of the page, below the eight thousand number, another number had been scrawled. She sucked in a breath. No. That couldn't mean what she thought it meant.

She raised her eyes to Scott's. "Minus thirty-seven thousand five hundred dollars?"

Scott nodded. "And do you see those initials beside it?"

Becky did. "EJ. Do you know what that means?"

Scott's lips tightened. "I sure do."

Scott paid for a general admission ticket to enter Keeneland. It was close to the end of the afternoon, probably only a couple of races left to run, but there was still a steady stream of race enthusiasts filing past the ticket window beneath the track's big stone entryway.

He stepped through the open breezeway, passed the gift shop, and joined a throng in the paddock. A line of horses were at that moment being ceremoniously paraded beneath the huge sycamores and maples that towered over the paddock as they made their way toward the saddle ring. Scott slipped into a gap in the crowd next to the metal railing to admire them. The next race was for fillies, and these magnificent beauties pranced in their eagerness to get on the track.

A line of jockeys arrived as the trainers started saddling the racers, eyeing their horses and each other, their expressions grim or stern as they assumed their game faces to meet the challenge ahead. A small cluster of well-dressed people stood a little distance from each horse to watch the saddle and review procedure. The owners and their guests.

Though he didn't spend much time at the track, Scott had to admit the atmosphere of excitement and anticipation stirred his blood. Gambling didn't appeal to him at all, but these horses were supreme athletes, every one of them. They loved to race, and always gave it their all. He'd seen horses suffer an injury and continue to run on three legs with every ounce of strength in them. Not many human athletes would be that dedicated.

Scott scanned the faces lining the black railing. He caught sight of several familiar ones, as he knew he would. Regulars during the months of April and October, when Keeneland's race meetings were held, racing forms clutched in their hands as they studied the horses, trying to decide which ones looked like winners. A beautiful little chestnut filly skittered sideways when her trainer tried to place the saddle on her back, and dozens of hands clutching pens made marks on their forms, noting her nervous energy.

Finally, Scott caught sight of the man on the other side of the paddock, standing with his back to the clubhouse. He stepped away from the railing and picked his way toward the tall, lanky man wearing a gray fedora and a pensive expression. He sidled up beside him and stood watching the number five horse for a moment.

"So who do you like in this one?" He didn't take his eyes off the horse as he spoke.

The man cast a quick glance his way. The corner of his mouth twitched. "Some fine-looking fillies there."

Scott nodded. "You're Eddie Jones, aren't you?"

He didn't seem concerned at being recognized by a stranger. Well, a man in his profession wouldn't.

"That's right. Have we met?"

"Not officially, but we've got mutual friends." Scott

turned to hold out his hand. "Scott Lewis, assistant manager out at Shady Acres."

Recognition flared in Eddie's face. "You work for Lee Courtney."

"And Zach Garrett." Scott watched the man's face as he dropped Zach's name. Mr. Courtney, though the more well-known of the two men, would certainly not have dealings with a man like Eddie Jones. But Zach had been known to place an occasional bet off-the-record.

Understanding showed in Eddie's eyes as he assumed he knew the reason for Scott's sudden introduction. That was, after all, the way bookies met their new customers, on the referral of others.

But Scott hadn't come to Keeneland to place an illegal bet. "Actually, I've taken over temporarily for Neal Haldeman at Out to Pasture."

The man's eyes flickered briefly at the mention of Haldeman, though his tone was carefully even. "I heard about that. Quite a shock."

"Yes, it was. I was hoping you might be able to answer a question or two."

"Why ask me? I don't know a thing about it, other than what I read in the paper."

Scott leaned forward and lowered his voice. "I've been going through some of Haldeman's records, and I found several—" he paused for effect, studying the man closely "—mentions of you in them."

Eddie's smile tightened as he returned Scott's gaze. "I'm not surprised."

Nor pleased, judging by the way the man's nostrils flared.

"I was just wondering how much Haldeman was into you for."

Eddie turned slightly away, his gaze going to the paddock where the number five horse was saddled and ready to be mounted. "I'd have to check."

Scott prodded. "Ballpark."

The man tapped pursed lips with a forefinger. "I'd say close to thirty." He looked back at Scott. "Why do you want to know?"

Scott held his gaze. "Just wondering whether this information is important enough to warrant turning it over to the police."

A bitter smile lifted the edges of his mouth. "Haldeman is no good to me dead, if that's what you're insinuating. A debt like this one isn't going to be paid out of his estate. Nor is it collectible from his relatives."

"No, but people like you have been known to apply pressure on occasion."

Anger flashed in the man's eyes. "Trust me, I wouldn't do someone in for thirty."

Scott held his hands out. "I'm not accusing you of anything. Just trying to get some answers."

He studied Scott for a moment. "I assume if you found mention of me, you found others, as well. Haldeman spread his business around pretty evenly. Word on the street is that he was down some fairly big numbers, all told."

Scott actually hadn't looked at Haldeman's files after his conversation with Becky. He'd wanted to get here before the last race. But he made a mental note to go through the rest of those tally sheets, see if he could find any other initials.

"My, my, my, look who's here."

Scott turned as the familiar female voice drawled in his ear. He shouldn't be surprised to see her here. She'd told them this morning she was on her way to the track.

"Miss Buchanan."

"Kaci, darling. Remember?" He took her outstretched hand, and she pressed it with her other one, her fingers rubbing in a caress over his skin as she had done this morning. Her gaze flickered over his shoulder. "Am I interrupting anything important?"

Scott flashed a quick look at Eddie, suddenly damp under the collar. He'd hate for anyone to think he was betting with a bookie. "No, nothing at all. We were just discussing a mutual friend."

Eddie eyed Kaci with a slick smile. "In fact, I was just leaving. Ma'am." He touched a finger to his hat before walking away. Scott thought he looked relieved to have an excuse to escape. He slipped into the crowd flowing toward the track and was quickly lost to sight.

Kaci lowered her voice, still clutching his hand. "I want to get up to the box for this race. But apparently I'm to have a visit from the police this evening." Her blue eyes caught his, her gaze hard.

"Really? Why?"

Her eyes moved as she searched his face. Then her mouth relaxed into a smile. "If it wasn't you, then it must have been Neal's secretary." Her voice dripped scorn at the mention of Becky. "The housekeeper called my cell phone about an hour ago to tell me the police stopped by with a few questions. Someone must have given them my name as a person of interest." Her smile stretched into a sly grin. "Of course, I am quite an interesting person, to those who get to know me."

Scott shifted his weight, suddenly uncomfortable. He wasn't used to females flirting so openly with him. "I'm sure you are," he managed.

The clear trumpet notes sounding the call to post cut through the murmur of the crowd, signalling the race was about to start. The speed of the people moving toward the track increased. Kaci glanced over Scott's shoulder.

"I must go. Mother's filly has a good chance of breaking her maiden in this one, and I don't want to miss it."

Scott gave her hand a final squeeze and released it. A racehorse's first win, or breaking its maiden, was a celebrated event among breeders and trainers alike. "Of course. Good luck to her."

Kaci fluttered her fingers in his direction and hurried toward the clubhouse elevator. Scott stood, indecisive, as the crowd surged around him. He could look for Eddie again, try to continue his conversation. But he didn't really need to. He'd gotten what he wanted from the guy, a verification of Haldeman's illegal betting activity, and a number.

The paddock area had emptied. Scott made his way toward the exit, remembering the flare of anger in Eddie's eyes and in his voice. True, thirty thousand dollars was probably not a big deal to a guy in Eddie's business. Not a big enough debt to kill a man over. But if Haldeman owed money to several people, and if each of them found out, it would certainly make someone worry that he wasn't going to get paid very quickly. He might want to apply a little pressure, to make sure his debt got settled first. And that kind of pressure could turn physical at the drop of a hat. Fistfights had been known to erupt for much less reason. And a fistfight could turn nasty quickly.

Especially if there was a handy weapon nearby.

# NINE

"Now boys, *please* be on your best behavior. We want to show our manners to Mr. Lewis, don't we?"

Becky eyed her sons in the rearview mirror as she turned into the driveway of the Pasture. Jamie, intent on the colorful plastic man in his hands, nodded obediently in answer to her request, but Tyler's face bore its usual stubborn expression.

"Why?"

Becky let out an exasperated sigh. "Because he's my new boss, and I want to make a good impression on him. I told you that."

The boy fixed her with a look so like his father's that Becky's heart stuttered in her chest. "Will he really fire you if me and Jamie act up?"

How could a child who had not seen his father since he was six months old speak in the same voice and look at her with Christopher's eyes? Genetics, she supposed. She lived in Christopher's shadow every day of her life. It just wasn't fair. Yet she loved these tiny replicas of their father more than she loved her own life.

She shoved the shifter into park. "You never know." She locked eyes with Tyler in the mirror. "He certainly won't be impressed with an assistant whose sons act like savages. He might not let me bring you back again."

She watched the dark head nod as he acknowledged the truth in her words, and breathed a sigh of relief. Her goal for this beautiful Saturday morning was to finish labeling the files for all that junk in Neal's drawer while the kids watched Saturday-morning cartoons on the TV. After she made up a few of the hours she missed Thursday afternoon, she'd promised the boys a trip to the park to feed the ducks.

Neal's truck still sat in the driveway, unmoved since Wednesday night. Today, Scott's truck was parked alongside it, and both the front and back barn doors stood open. Neal usually left the front doors closed. A small difference, but one that served as a reminder that Neal was no longer in charge of Out to Pasture.

The moment she turned the key and cut the engine, the boys tumbled out the back doors and took off at a run toward the barn. Becky gathered her purse, watching through the windshield as Sam greeted them, his tail whipping back and forth while they petted and hugged him. She opened the car door, her pulse speeding up when Scott stepped to the wide barn doorway to meet her sons.

"Hello, there! You must not be strangers, or my guard dog wouldn't be licking your faces."

"Sam knows us." Jamie stared at him with serious eyes. "He's our friend."

Scott grinned at her, but he answered Jamie with utmost seriousness. "I can see that."

Jamie stood straight and stuck out a hand. "Pleased to meet you. I'm Jamie Dennison."

Becky hid a smile. At least Jamie had listened to her

lecture on manners this morning. Maybe Tyler would follow his brother's lead.

Scott returned Jamie's greeting formally. "Nice to meet you, Jamie. I'm Scott Lewis."

When Scott released his hand, Tyler shoved his forward. "I'm Tyler. Are you going to fire my mom if I act like a savage?"

With a groan, Becky leaned against the hood of her car and shook her head. Out of the corner of her eye she saw Scott considering his answer. "Probably not," he told Tyler, "but I might ask her to keep you in the office so you won't get in my way out here. Only big kids who behave themselves can help with the horses, you know."

Tyler's face lit with excitement at the suggestion of helping with the horses. "I'm a big kid. I'm in kindergarten."

Scott grinned at her over the tops of two dark heads. "Good. I can use some helpers today."

Becky opened her mouth to protest. She didn't come to work on a Saturday to play with horses. She had things to do in the office. And she couldn't dump the boys on Scott while she went inside.

Her protest died unspoken as a car pulled into the driveway. The sunlight gleamed on the polished hood of a gold Mercedes Roadster. It slowed to a stop midway down the driveway, the sun's rays reflecting off the windshield so that Becky couldn't see the driver clearly. She glanced at Scott, who shrugged.

Becky approached the driver's door and stopped beside the tinted windows. After a moment, the window opened a few inches, revealing a woman in large dark sunglasses with a tan print scarf covering her head.

Odd. Sometimes people came on Saturdays for a tour,

but she hadn't made note on the calendar of anyone scheduled for today. Maybe this woman was out for a drive and stopped in when she saw the sign by the road.

"Hello." Becky dipped her head toward the window. "Are you here for a tour?"

The dark glasses hid most of the woman's face, but her lips, unadorned with lipstick, tightened into a crooked line for a moment before she answered. "No. I…uh, no."

Was that a sob that broke her voice? Becky couldn't be sure, but the skin on her arm prickled with sudden suspicion. Could this woman be the mysterious "L"? Maybe the owner of the footprint returning to check out the scene of her crime?

"What can we do for you, Ms.…." She let her tone rise, an unspoken request for the stranger's name.

"Keller." The woman's lips snapped shut. She faced forward, staring through the windshield at the place where Scott and the boys stood near the entrance to the barn, watching them.

The boys! Fear clawed at Becky's throat. What had possessed her to bring the boys here today? Neal's killer was still on the loose, and maybe even sitting here now, with her fancy car pointed directly toward them.

The woman drew a shuddering breath and spoke without facing Becky, the eyes invisible behind the glasses. "I… I just wanted to look around, if that's okay?"

A sob stuttered her voice. That sounded like genuine grief. Becky took a step toward the window, her suspicions beginning to fade. Did killers grieve over their victims? The scarf was knotted beneath an untidy mass of dark hair at the back of her head. The woman's rather large nose was red, the nostrils rubbed nearly raw. Either she was suffering from a bad cold, or she had recently indulged in a violent crying spell. A shuddering breath gave evidence of the latter, and compassion warred with suspicion in Becky. Maybe she wasn't a killer after all. A friend of Neal's, perhaps?

"I don't know if Mr. Lewis has time to conduct a tour this morning." She cast a glance toward Scott.

The woman killed the engine and got out of the car. When she stood, she towered a full head over Becky. That wasn't unusual. Most people did.

Scott stepped forward, the boys and Sam tagging along. He held out his hand. "Hello, I'm Scott Lewis. I'm taking care of things around here for a little while."

The woman's hand froze in the process of stretching out to take Scott's, and a sob escaped her lips. Her shoulders hunched forward and her hands rose to cover her face, glasses and all, as she succumbed to a fit of weeping.

"Oh, you poor thing." All her suspicions melting at the sight of the woman's grief, Becky rushed forward and put an arm around the sobbing woman's shoulders.

The boys stood openmouthed. A grown woman blubbering like a child wasn't something they saw often. Becky squeezed the shuddering shoulders and made soothing noises while Scott watched, his extended hand clenching and unclenching.

After a moment, the woman pulled a much-used tissue from the pocket of her jacket and scrubbed at her red nose. "I'm suh-sorry to act like a fool. I just—" Another heave robbed her of words and she shook her head violently, knocking her glasses lopsided on her face. She shoved them up to perch on top of her scarf like the eyes of a giant insect.

Grief could ravage the looks of even a beautiful woman, and this woman was no beauty to begin with. Despair had wreaked havoc on her face. She folded the ragged tissue and attempted to blot at her eyes, the lids of which were so reddened and swollen that discerning their normal shape was impossible.

With a huge intake of breath, she shoved the damp scrap of tissue back in her pocket and thrust her hand toward Scott in a belated greeting. "Please forgive me for being rude, Mr. Lewis. My name is Isabelle Keller, and I'm a…" Becky thought she might sob again, but instead she swallowed hard and continued with obvious difficulty. "I was a friend of Neal Haldeman."

Isabelle Keller. Becky knew that name. Isabelle's father was a well-known real estate mogul who had bought and sold half the land in central Kentucky at one time or other. His name was in the newspaper almost every day. Becky had spoken with Isabelle on the phone several times, and had overheard Neal arranging to pick her up for dinner just last week. At the time Becky had noted that his attitude on the phone was deferential, unlike his tone when he spoke with women like Kaci Buchanan.

Neal had certainly moved in lofty circles.

Becky placed a hand on the woman's arm. "Miss Keller, I'm so sorry for your loss. Please accept my condolences." Isabelle's lips twisted in her effort to hold back another sob. "I'm Becky Dennison, Neal's assistant."

Recognition cleared the lines from her forehead and she took Becky's hand. Becky kept her expression kind as she returned the woman's troubled gaze.

"I remember. Neal said—" She stopped, struggling to maintain her composure, then continued. "Neal said you were a big help to him, that you were going to organize things in the office. He was so glad to have you." Fresh tears pooled in her eyes. Fumbling in her pocket, she withdrew the abused scrap of tissue again. "I'm so sorry. I didn't think anyone would be here today."

"Mommy?" Jamie edged toward her, his gaze fixed on Isabelle as he laid a hand on Becky's leg. His loud whisper rasped over the sound of the woman's sniffle. "What's wrong with that lady?"

"Jamie." Becky infused her tone with warning as her stern expression told her son to hold his tongue.

Scott cleared his throat. "Tell you what, boys. I could use some help feeding the horses. Think you guys could give me a hand?"

"Wow!" Tyler ran toward her, bouncing on his toes. "Can we, Mommy? Please?"

Becky lifted her gaze from their pleading faces to Scott's. The twins could be a handful, and she really hadn't intended to dump them on her boss. Scott nodded almost imperceptibly toward Isabelle and then the house. Obviously, he'd rather deal with them than a crying woman.

Becky laid a hand on each boy's shoulder. "Okay, but only if you promise to do exactly what Mr. Lewis says. And no fighting. And no standing up on the golf cart."

Jamie's eyes lit up. "We get to ride on the golf cart?"

"Woo-hoo!" Tyler pumped a fist into the air.

Scott nodded toward Isabelle and then with an unmistakable air of relief, headed toward the barn, flanked by excitedly leaping boys.

Becky smiled into Isabelle's tear-streaked face. "Perhaps you'd like to come inside. I can put on a pot of coffee, or maybe make some tea."

Isabelle hesitated. "Tea would be good, if it's herbal."

"It is."

Becky placed an assuring arm around her and guided her toward the back door. Inside, she steered Isabelle into the kitchen and gestured toward a seat at the small table in the center of the room. She ran hot water into the large glass measuring cup she used to make her own tea every morning. While that heated in the microwave, she placed a boxed assortment of herbal teas on the table and got two clean mugs from the cupboard. She set the unchipped one in front of Isabelle.

A comfortable silence, broken only by the occasional sniffle, descended between them as they each selected a pouch from the box. When the microwave dinged, Becky poured water over Isabelle's tea bag, and peach-scented steam rose from her mug. She retrieved a box of tissues from the office, which drew a brief smile of thanks from her distraught guest.

As Isabelle stirred a package of sweetener into her mug, Becky dunked her tea bag rhythmically in the steaming water. The sharp odor of mint from her mug mingled with the peach. She kept her gaze on the swiftly darkening tea. "Have you known Neal a long time?"

"We met at a Christmas party." Isabelle reached for a fresh tissue as she shook her head. "Four months ago. It seems much longer."

There could be only one possible reason for such grief for a man she'd known such a short time. Becky swirled her tea bag and spoke softly. "Were you in love with him?"

More tears rolled unchecked down her red cheeks as Isabelle nodded. "From the first moment. He was so handsome and funny. And passionate." She looked up quickly. "About the horses, I mean. He told me all about them, and he spoke as though they were his children."

"In a way, I think they were."

A brief smile took her lips. "That's what Father said. But that's only because—" She bit back whatever she'd been about to say with a hard swallow.

Becky pulled the tea bag from her mug and sipped, breathing in the sweet odor of wintergreen. She judged the woman to be in her early thirties, not much older than Becky. "His death must have come as such a shock."

She nodded miserably. "We were to have dinner Thursday night, a special dinner. When he didn't arrive to pick me up, I thought—" She broke off and stared into her mug. When she continued, her voice was soft. "Father said it wouldn't last, that Neal was only interested in me because of money. He forbade me to give him any." Her tear-filled eyes rose to lock with Becky's. "But he never asked. Not once since the night we met. So he couldn't have been after my money, could he?" Her voice held a note of desperation.

Though she'd only worked with Neal two months, Becky had seen him pursue donations for the Pasture with charming single-mindedness. Would he have dated a woman only to get money for his precious horses? Possibly. But only temporarily, perhaps a dinner date or two. Surely he wouldn't continue a relationship for months under false pretenses.

Becky blew the steam from her tea and sipped, aware that Isabelle waited fearfully for her answer. Neal was gone, and there was no reason for the poor woman to wonder for the rest of her life whether the man she loved had loved her in return. Tears of sympathy stung her eyes, and she replied with a confidence she didn't feel. "Of course not. Neal had too much integrity for that."

Isabelle seemed to draw comfort from her certainty. Her mug still untouched, she leaned against the back of the chair. "If only Father had known him better. And he would have had the opportunity soon."

Her mouth snapped shut. She clutched the mug with both hands and hesitated, clearly holding back something. Becky remained silent, confident that given the opportunity, whatever Isabelle had to say would spill forth.

The woman's gaze rose to meet with Becky's. "Neal would have made a wonderful father. I know he would."

Staring into the mournful dark eyes, Becky's jaw went slack. What was she saying?

"Isabelle, are you pregnant?"

Isabelle's chin trembled as she nodded. "I know it was soon, and we didn't plan for this to happen. I planned to tell Neal that night. Then he didn't show up for our date, and he didn't answer his phone. I didn't sleep at all, worrying that he'd found out about the baby and was angry with me. Which was silly, I know, because no one knows except me, but I couldn't imagine why he would stand me up. Then I read yesterday's paper."

She broke down again, deep sobs racking her body as she drooped over the table. Becky lifted the hot tea mug out of harm's way and laid a hand on her arm. What could she say? She knew no words of comfort equal to this woman's devastating circumstance.

After a moment the sobbing eased and Isabelle raised her head. This time she sipped the warm tea Becky pushed toward her, and as she did her tears quieted.

"What will you do?"

Isabelle drew a deep breath. "I'll raise our baby alone. Father will be furious when I tell him. He may even throw me out." She lifted her chin. "If he does, I'll get a job. I went to college. Surely someone will hire me."

Becky hoped she was right. She knew all too well the trials in store for a mother struggling to raise her children alone. It was certainly a different life from the one Isabelle enjoyed now, with her Mercedes and her rich father.

She reached across the table to cover Isabelle's hand with her own. "You'll be in my prayers."

The woman blinked, and then her features softened. "Thank you."

# TEN

Scott steered the boys toward the barn. He glanced backward and felt like a couple of cement blocks had been lifted off his chest at the sight of Becky and Isabelle Keller disappearing through the office door. Thank goodness Becky had arrived before the weepy heiress.

"Was that lady sad?"

Both boys watched him with round, dark eyes and solemn expressions. They looked a lot alike, enough that they might be mistaken for one another at a quick glance. But when he looked closer, Scott saw that the one who introduced himself as Tyler was a little taller, and Jamie's face was more slender. And thank goodness Becky didn't dress them alike. Jamie wore a red nylon ski jacket, and his brother an electric-blue one.

Tyler shoved his brother's shoulder. "Duh, stupid. Why else would she be crying?"

Jamie rounded on him, anger blazing in his eyes. "Don't push me, Tyler. Mommy said not to fight."

Scott stepped forward and looked down on both of them, taking advantage of his intimidating height to forestall a scuffle. "If you're going to fight, you'll have to go in the house with the women. I can't have you upsetting the horses."

Eyes wide, they both nodded. Scott addressed Jamie. "Yes, I think that lady was sad. She must have known Mr. Haldeman." He snapped his mouth shut. What had Becky told her sons about Haldeman's death? Better to keep quiet than to say anything that might confuse them.

The edges of Jamie's mouth drooped. "I don't like it when ladies cry. It makes me upset."

Out of the mouths of babes. Scott glanced toward the back door of the house before nodding at Jamie. "Me, too."

He stepped into the barn, the boys and Sam following. He picked up the pouch into which he'd placed the various morning medications that needed to be administered.

"Shotgun!" Tyler sprinted across the dirt floor.

Jamie raced behind him. "No fair! I want to ride up front."

"Too bad." Tyler leaped onto the cart's front bench, and smirked at his brother. "I called shotgun first."

Did they argue like this all the time? Scott hadn't been blessed with brothers, and his only sister was six years older. When they were kids he liked to pester her, of course, but they never really fought. She would have squashed him like a bug.

"Nobody gets shotgun." He let his stern gaze slide from Jamie to Tyler. "Except Sam. That's his seat."

Tyler pouted for a second, but then shrugged and climbed over the seat back to the bench that faced the rear of the cart. Scott hefted the bag of feed he'd filled earlier and deposited it on the floorboard in the front. Jamie climbed up beside his brother.

"Up here, Sam." He slid behind the steering wheel and patted the bench. The dog leaped up to stand on the seat, then began licking the back of both boys' heads. Grinning at their laughter, Scott guided the cart through the barn and out the back door.

The warm sunlight dazzled his eyes, but a cool breeze still held a latent trace of winter as it blew the scent of sweet hay into his face. He buttoned the collar of his denim jacket and eyed the fencing as he steered between the paddocks. The top plank on his left would need to be replaced soon; Rusty had done a number on it. Since he had read through all the files concerning the stallions' diets, he knew the horse didn't have a mineral deficiency. He was probably just bored. Scott made a mental note to spray the fence with Chew Stop and to check Rusty's mouth for splinters.

He halted the cart beside Gadsby's feed bucket. The boys and Sam leaped to the ground as the gelding caught sight of them and trotted across the grass in their direction.

"Wow, look at him!" Jamie's eyes grew round as Gadsby neared. "He's a giant horse."

Tyler propped a foot on the bottom fence rail and, with a hand on his hip, spoke with authority to his brother. "He's not a giant. He's regular size. Isn't he, Mr. Lewis?"

Scott eyed the horse. "He's good-sized, but he's not a giant."

Tyler leveled a smirk on Jamie. "Told you."

Scott opened the top of the bag and grabbed the scoop. "He is a movie star, though."

"Wow." Jamie eyed Gadsby with awe. "What movie was he in?"

Scott emptied the scoop into the bucket, then added a second. "*Seabiscuit.* It's about a famous racehorse from a long time ago. You should ask your mom to rent it for you. It's a good story, and you'll see Gadsby."

"Gadsby. That's a great name." Admiration flooded Tyler's voice as he gazed on the happily munching horse.

His hand rose, but halted just outside the fence as he looked up at Scott. "Does he care if I touch him?"

Scott hesitated. Gadsby was one of the gentler horses in residence at the Pasture, but no sense taking chances. "In a minute, when he finishes eating."

The boys nodded, and they all watched as Gadsby chewed. The cool morning air seemed to magnify the sounds of the horse's teeth grinding the fiber. The sunlight gleamed on the smooth lines of his back and turned his coat a deep auburn.

"Gadsby is what's called blood bay," he told the boys, "because his coat is that rich, red color. And you see the way his mane, tail and the lower part of his legs are darker? Those are called dark points."

Jamie, far more cautious than his brother, eased up to the fence beside Tyler, his gaze fixed on Gadsby. "You're smart about horses, aren't you?"

Grinning, Scott ruffled his hair. "I've learned a few things. I've been around them since I was younger than you."

Two pastures away, Bull called toward them with an impatient whinny. Toward the front of the farm, Fortune answered. Everybody was hungry this morning.

"I wish we had a horse." Tyler leaped off the bottom plank and ran over to the golf cart. "Can I feed the next one?"

"Don't you want to pet Gadsby when he finishes eating?"

The boy shrugged. "He takes too long."

Scott shook his head. The kid had the attention span of a Chihuahua. "Okay, let's get moving. Yes, you can feed the next one." Jamie's mouth opened, and Scott spoke before he could complain. "They get two scoops, so you can each do one."

He climbed up in the golf cart and waited for Sam to settle beside him before releasing the brake.

As the cart rolled forward, Tyler shoved a hand into the air. "I'm first."

"No fair!"

Scott heaved a sigh.

When Becky followed a much calmer Isabelle through the back door, a flash of fluorescent green whizzed within a few inches of her head and bounced off the doorjamb. Startled, she threw her hands up to protect her face. A blur of yellow fur zoomed by her.

"Sorry, Mommy!"

From across the yard, Tyler turned a guilty grin her way as Sam retrieved the tennis ball and bounded toward him.

She leveled a frown on her son. "Young man, you've got to be more careful. That almost hit the glass. And me."

He ducked his head, then raced after the dog to try to wrestle the ball out of his mouth, Jamie running after them. At least they were both getting a lot of exercise today, running in the yard with Sam. Maybe tonight they'd go to sleep early.

Scott left his position near the barn and crossed the driveway as Becky followed Isabelle to her car.

Clutching her sunglasses, the heiress took a step toward him. "Mr. Lewis, I hope you'll forgive my earlier behavior."

Scott shoved his hands into his jeans pockets. "No apologies necessary, ma'am. I'm sorry for, uh, your loss." He shot a quick glance at Becky, a clear plea for rescue.

Hiding a smile, she stepped forward and took Isabelle's slim hand in hers. "Good luck. Don't forget, I'm here if you need someone to talk to."

The woman's smile wavered, but she held on to her composure. "Thank you. For everything."

She slid into the Mercedes, but before she shut the door she looked out over the paddocks. Then she directed a trembling smile toward them. "Goodbye."

Scott moved forward to stand beside Becky as the car backed onto the road and then pulled away. A bird in a branch overhead scolded when they walked beneath a thickly leafed sugar maple toward the boys.

"I guess she was upset about Haldeman." Scott's statement held a question.

Becky nodded. "She's in love with him."

"With Haldeman?" Disbelief twisted his features.

Sam raced by them as they reached the edge of the driveway, the boys hot on his trail, shrieking with laughter.

"Why do you say it like that?"

He watched the boys romping in the grass. "I wouldn't think Haldeman was the type to appeal to a rich heiress like her."

"Well, he did. And apparently the feeling was mutual."

Scott's gaze slid sideways, skeptical. "I find that even harder to believe. If he was in love with Isabelle Keller, why was Kaci Buchannan dropping earrings in his sofa?"

Tyler caught up with the dog and threw both arms around his neck to restrain him while Jamie pried the ball out of his mouth. Becky watched her sons, struggling to come up with a plausible explanation in Isabelle's favor.

"Neal wouldn't want to be rude to Kaci," she said slowly. "She's too prominent."

Scott snorted a laugh. "You mean she's too rich."

"Isabelle is rich, too. At least, her father is."

Scott lifted a shoulder. "Yes, but Kaci is beautiful as well as rich."

Anger flared on behalf of her new friend. At least, she

hoped that was the reason. She still felt a bit of antagonism toward Kaci, the arrogant blonde.

"Beauty is more than looks. Apparently Neal recognized that." She snapped her jaw shut.

He twisted his head to stare at her, surprise coloring his features. "She really made an impression on you. What did she say to make you defend her like this?"

Becky watched the boys a moment before answering. Jamie held the ball high above his head, clutched in a white-fingered grip, while Sam sat patiently in front of him, his stare fixed on his toy. Finally Jamie threw it, and then wiped his hand on his jeans as the dog raced across the yard in hot pursuit.

"I guess I just feel sorry for her." She glanced at Scott, then away again. "She's pregnant with Neal's child."

Scott gave a low whistle. "That must have been a shock."

"Neal didn't know. Isabelle was going to tell him the night he was killed."

"I didn't mean Neal." He pivoted on his boots to peer at her. "How much do you know about her father, Mr. Keller?"

"I know he's rich. He's in the paper all the time."

"Yeah, and did you catch that article about him a few weeks ago?"

Becky knew the one he meant. "One of his employees accused him of assault."

"That's the one." He shoved a hand in his jeans pocket. "Apparently that wasn't the first time he's been accused of slugging an employee, but nothing ever comes of it. I thought at the time that the guy making the accusation would probably drop the whole thing and get a big check in return."

They stood in silence. Sam's excited barking sounded

loud against the backdrop of a distant whinny from the pasture across the street. Becky battled guilt as she watched Tyler toss the ball high into the air. Why hadn't she kept her mouth shut? What a lousy friend she turned out to be.

And what if Isabelle's father was angry with her? If he hit his employees, was he the kind of man who would hit his daughter? Or her lover?

"Whoa!" Scott took off at a run.

Startled, Becky looked after him. Her heart skipped a beat when she saw the tennis ball bounce inside Alidor's paddock. Sam, well trained by Neal, didn't go after the ball but stood obediently on this side of the fence. Tyler raced across the grass, his little legs pumping as hard as he could push them. From the far side of the paddock, the fiery stallion noticed the new object in his territory and started to run toward it.

"Don't go in there!"

Thankfully, Tyler stopped when Scott shouted. He turned a question-filled face toward him, but then stepped backward as Alidor arrived at the tennis ball and blew a loud snort. The stallion tossed his head and pawed at the ball.

Scott came to a stop beside Tyler and put a hand on his shoulder. His voice carried back to her. "Alidor doesn't like it when strangers go in his paddock. I found that out the other day. Let's see if we can find another tennis ball for Sam. I'll get that one later, when there aren't so many people around to upset him."

Jamie fell into step beside them as they headed toward the barn, but peeled off to come toward her. "I'm hungry."

Becky glanced at her watch. Eleven-ten. "You should have eaten more breakfast. It's not lunchtime yet."

"Actually," said Scott, giving her a sheepish smile, "I'm

kind of hungry myself. You interested in grabbing a hamburger somewhere?"

"Yeah!" Tyler ran to her side. "Please, Mommy?"

Becky's throat closed around any words she might have tried to force out. Was Scott offering to take them out? No, better not assume that. He was probably just suggesting a friendly lunch, Dutch treat. Unfortunately, she couldn't afford a restaurant, not even fast food.

"I have peanut butter sandwiches in the car." She didn't look at Scott's face, too embarrassed to claim poverty. "Remember our picnic at the park, boys?"

"We're gonna feed the ducks," Jamie informed him.

From the corner of her eye she saw Scott shrug. "Peanut butter keeps. And I think Sam would love to go to the park after lunch and chase a few ducks."

She looked up, and her pulse danced when he smiled into her eyes. This good-looking man actually wanted to spend his Saturday afternoon with her *and* her boys? Either they'd behaved themselves better than she could have hoped while she was inside, or he found her…

No. She wouldn't go there. He probably just didn't want to sit around the Pasture alone all afternoon.

She found herself nodding, and the twins let out a yelp of delight. How much could a burger cost, anyway?

# ELEVEN

Scott pulled the truck into the Pasture's driveway. He parked, then threw back his head and gave in to a jaw-stretching yawn. He'd always been an early bird, but five o'clock on Sunday morning was stretching the point, even for him.

Somebody had to feed the horses, though, and they needed their morning medication. Life on the farm didn't stop just because it was the Lord's day.

"And somebody has to feed the dog, too, huh, fella?"

Sam lifted his head off the bench seat, and his tail thumped sluggishly. Even the dog thought five o'clock was too early. He'd follow Scott around on his morning chores, and then probably take a snooze in the barn while Scott attended church.

He got out of the truck and clutched his jacket together as a cold predawn wind whipped it open. He ducked his head to shield his neck with his collar and trotted toward the house with Sam on his heels.

He twisted the handle on the storm door, fumbling with his keys. Gripping the correct one, he extended it toward the inside door—

And stopped.

The inside door stood open. He stared at it, thoughts

spinning. Did Becky close it yesterday? Yes, he remembered standing by the truck, waiting for Jamie to run inside and grab his backpack. When the boy ran out, Becky pulled it closed and locked it with her key. He didn't open the house at all last night when he came back to the Pasture, just the barn.

He stepped forward through the door to get a look at the handle. Yeah, it was scarred and bent. Somebody jimmied the lock.

What could they hope to steal from the office of a nonprofit organization like the Pasture?

Whatever they were after, they'd ransacked the place. The front room was a wreck. The couch cushions had been slashed open, as was the pathetic old armchair in the corner. The brochure rack had been thrown to the floor and the contents scattered everywhere. Odd, though. The television and DVD player were still in place. Not a random burglary, then. From where he stood he could just see a corner of the office, the floor littered with papers. All Becky's work organizing the contents of Haldeman's desk, wasted.

Sam pushed past him and headed for the kitchen.

"Sam, come."

The dog reluctantly returned. They stepped outside, and Scott unclipped his cell phone to call the police.

The hallways of Grace Community Church were filled with Sunday morning worshippers. Becky kept her voice pitched low as she glanced over Amber's shoulder to be sure no one overheard. "And after lunch, he spent a couple of hours at the park with us." A steady stream of people filed past them through the busy church hallway on their way to the sanctuary.

She felt like a teenager giggling over a guy with her friend, but a girl needed someone to bounce things off. After Scott insisted on buying their lunch at McDonald's, she'd been going crazy trying to decide if it was just a friendly gesture on his part, or if she'd actually been on a date.

"How did the boys act around him?" With a hand on her arm, Amber moved her against the wall to let a group of green-robed choir members pass. "Did they seem jealous?"

"Not at all. Except of each other. They both kept trying to monopolize Scott's attention." A smile curved Becky's lips as she remembered Jamie parading each of his men out for a personal introduction to Scott. "They obviously liked him a lot."

Amber frowned. "That's not good."

"It's not?"

"You don't want them to appear desperate for male attention. That will drive him away as quickly as a clingy woman."

Becky hadn't thought of that. Amber's logic made sense, though. Neediness in any form was a guaranteed man repellent.

"I don't see what I can do about that." The crowd thinned to a few stragglers, and they headed slowly for the sanctuary doors as the first strains of the organ prelude reverberated through the church. "They are desperate for male attention, poor things."

Amber drummed her fingers on her Bible as they walked. "The next thing to do is get him alone. Let him see that you're a self-assured woman, totally at peace with yourself and your singleness." She peered sideways at Becky. "You can do that, can't you?"

At peace with her singleness? Until a few days ago Becky would have answered, "Absolutely!" But since Scott took over at the Pasture, her decision to remain single after her divorce five years ago was wavering.

Becky met her friend's gaze with a hesitant grimace. "Maybe."

Amber's eyebrows shot upward, but her whispered response was drowned out by the organ's chords. As they entered the sanctuary they passed the acolyte, a cherub-faced girl in white who stood like a statue, holding the candlelighter for an usher's match. Becky followed Amber down the center aisle to slip into a half-empty pew on the left.

Becky placed her purse beside her feet and settled onto the hard pew. She leaned over and whispered in Amber's ear. "Where's Jeff? I thought he'd be saving us a seat."

"He got called in to work this morning. A robbery or something."

Becky nodded, then faced the front of the sanctuary. Something else she'd spent a considerable amount of time considering last night was whether or not to tell Jeff this morning about Isabelle Keller. The decision to report Kaci Buchanan had been a no-brainer. No matter what Scott said, Kaci's visit to the Pasture for that earring looked suspicious.

The choir filed into the loft from a door to the right of the baptistry. A sudden swell of the organ's music indicated the end of the prelude. Beside her, Amber picked up two hymnals from the pew in front of them and handed one to Becky with a smile. Becky nodded her thanks and flipped the book open, her thoughts far from the morning's worship service.

Isabelle's visit, on the other hand, was a perfectly natural move for a grief-stricken woman. Nothing at all of interest for the police.

Even so, she felt a flood of relief at Jeff's absence this morning.

* * *

Scott shifted on the seat cushion as the screen behind Pastor Greg's head changed to display his third and, hopefully, final sermon point. The man next to him glanced his way, and Scott flashed an apologetic smile. He couldn't force himself to concentrate on the message this morning, but at least he could sit quietly so he didn't distract others.

He should probably have stayed at the Pasture while the police combed through the house. But he'd answered all their questions as best he could, then they shooed him away. After the horses had been fed and doctored, there wasn't much for him to do except stand around in the barn and watch the stream of police officers going in and out of the house. When Trooper Whitley told him he might as well go home, he'd jumped at the chance to leave. A good worship service was just what he needed today.

Unfortunately, the praise music had failed to direct his attention where it should be, to the Lord. And Pastor Greg might as well have been chanting in Latin for all Scott was getting out of his sermon.

What could a thief have been after? The only thing he'd noticed missing for sure was the petty cash box, but Becky kept less than fifty dollars in there. Of course, a thief wouldn't necessarily know that. Whitley and Detective Foster refused to talk about it, but another officer mentioned the possibility that a burglar had read of Haldeman's death in the newspaper and knew the house would be empty. That made sense, but a shadowy doubt niggled at Scott. Why hadn't the television and DVD player been taken? There was more to this than the cops were admitting.

The break-in wasn't the only thing on Scott's mind this

morning. Despite his determination not to fidget he shifted on the seat again, drawing another glance from his neighbor.

Why did he offer to take Becky and the boys out to lunch yesterday? He'd been set for a solitary afternoon in the office, going through Haldeman's records to see if he could discover the extent of the man's gambling debt. Instead, he ended up throwing stale crackers to a flock of fat ducks and teaching kids to hand-walk across the monkey bars.

He smiled, remembering Tyler's victory dance when he made it all the way to the other side unassisted. Jamie, the less athletic of the two, couldn't manage to get past five rungs before dropping to the ground. But he had an incredible mind for detail, and his face came alive as he told the stories behind about forty of those toys he carried around in his backpack.

Becky had done a great job raising those two, if Scott was any judge. Sure, they argued a lot, and occasionally even got physical with each other. But she was quick to step in, and he could see they respected her.

He crossed his right leg over his left, shifting away from the man beside him. He'd enjoyed the afternoon more than he expected. Especially Becky. She wasn't one of those women who watched from the sidelines. No, she got right in there and tried to cross the monkey bars, too. She didn't make it even as far as Jamie, but she faced her failure with a laugh and good grace.

It couldn't be easy raising two boys alone. She spoke of her father living out in California, and said she didn't have any other relatives close by. She never mentioned her ex-husband, but according to Trooper Whitley, he left when the boys were babies.

Thoughts of Becky's ex conjured up another memory,

one he'd prefer to forget. Megan, her face streaked with tears, begging him to understand why she was returning to her ex-husband, to her marriage. A wave of the familiar pain threatened to latch on to him again, but he fought against it, crossing his arms over his chest. She'd sworn the marriage was over, that it had ended long before the divorce made it final.

She'd lied.

Movement at the front of the room interrupted Scott's thoughts. The worship team stepped into position to play the final song as Pastor Greg invited the congregation to join him in a closing prayer. Scott uncrossed his legs and leaned forward. But though he bowed his head and closed his eyes, his thoughts refused to follow the pastor's words. His own turmoil tumbled out in a private prayer.

*Lord, I know I swore I'd never again get involved with a divorced woman.*

That oath was two years old, and he had remained true to his vow. In fact, the desire to date anyone seemed to have left along with Megan. The pain of his broken heart lingered. He wasn't about to risk another disaster. Every time he considered asking a woman out, that ache in his heart made it easy to walk away.

Until yesterday.

*Lord, Becky is different. She's alone, like I am. So if You—*

Music cut into his private prayer. The pastor must have said Amen, but he didn't hear it. Scott scrambled to his feet along with the rest of the congregation and returned the smile of an older woman across the aisle. Words to one of his favorite praise choruses projected onto the screen. He closed his eyes and added his voice to those of his fellow worshippers.

As he reached out with his heart and his hands toward his heavenly Father, peace washed over him. He wasn't alone in this. When the time was right, he'd know whether Becky was the one God had picked out for him or not.

# TWELVE

$B$ecky fought against a sudden attack of nerves as she pulled into the driveway for work Monday morning. Amber's words echoed in her mind. *Let him see that you're a self-assured woman, at peace with your singleness.* At the moment she felt neither self-assured nor at peace. In fact, the fluttering in her stomach made her want to throw up.

She caught sight of Scott inside the barn, standing at the workbench with his back toward her. When she cut the engine, music from his radio seeped through the shut windows of her car. The volume must be high enough that he didn't hear her arrive. Clutching the steering wheel with both hands, she closed her eyes and spent a moment bolstering her nerve.

*There's nothing needy about me. I'm self-assured. At peace with my singleness.*

And she really should be, too. This thing with Scott would probably lead to nothing, and that was best. It was absolutely nuts to become romantically involved with the boss. Everybody knew that. If it didn't work out, she'd be the one looking for a job, not him.

But he certainly was easy to be with. And he seemed to genuinely enjoy spending time with the boys Saturday.

Most single men ran screaming at the mention of one child, but two? And twins? She couldn't forget that the whole outing had been Scott's idea, not hers.

Regardless, she couldn't sit in the car all day. If he turned around and saw her staring at him, he wouldn't think she was needy. He'd think she was strange.

Gathering her purse and lunch bag from the passenger seat, she opened the car door and stood. Sam bounded out of the barn, tail flapping like a flag in a tornado.

"Good morning," she shouted toward the barn as she stooped to greet the dog.

Scott whirled, his face lighting with a smile that brought a warm flush to hers. "Hey, Becky. I didn't hear you." He leaned across the workbench to flip the radio off, then came toward her, wiping his hands on a dirty rag that probably did more harm than good. "How was your Sunday?"

"Good. Relaxing." She hefted her purse strap onto her shoulder. "Yours?"

His lips twisted sideways for a moment before he answered. "Interesting. We had a little excitement here yesterday."

"Oh?" She looked out across the paddocks and their peacefully grazing occupants. Everything appeared to be normal.

"Yeah. I almost called you at home, but the police didn't think it was necessary."

"The police?" Her eyes widened. "No one else has been hurt, have they?"

He shook his head. "Nothing like that. The office was broken into Saturday night."

"Oh, no! What did they take?"

"The petty cash box is about all I could see. The place is pretty much a shambles, though. They went through both desks, dumped everything out. I tried to clean up yesterday afternoon." He ducked his head. "It's still a mess, I'm afraid."

Becky's hand flew to her collarbone. A thief went through her desk? She mentally reviewed the contents. Thank goodness she didn't keep anything of any personal value in there. Still, to have someone going through her desk left her feeling violated.

"The checkbook!" She put a hand on his arm. "Oh, Scott, I keep the Pasture's checkbook and bank statements in my desk."

"They were still there." He covered her hand with his warm one, and she tried to ignore the thrill that shot up her arm. "I found all that stuff on the floor. But I still think we need to contact the bank this morning, tell them what's happened and maybe even close the account. Just in case they got the account number."

She shot him a quick smile and pulled her hand away. "I'll do that."

"Thanks. I started trying to put things back in folders, but I couldn't figure out what went where." He grimaced. "I just piled everything on your desk for you to sort out."

She couldn't help laughing at the chagrin on his face, and her nerves steadied a little. "Don't worry about it. I'll take care of things in there." She pulled a face. "I suppose there's fingerprint powder all over the place again?"

"I'm afraid so."

She heaved a sigh. "Great. I'm going to need a new bottle of cleaner soon."

"Oh, that reminds me." He pulled a crumpled piece of paper out of his back pocket. "Before all this happened I made a list of things we need to do this week. Some meds and other supplies are running low, and I'd like to get Doc Matthews out here to take a look at Kiri's Kousin. There are a couple of lesions on his flank region that I hope aren't ringworm."

He was suddenly all business. Her gaze dropped to the paper he thrust toward her. Was he going to completely ignore Saturday? A flicker of disappointment threatened to melt her smile. Okay, she could do that.

She started toward the house, nodding. "I'll give him a call as soon as his office opens. Anything else?"

"Remember those tally sheets of Haldeman's?"

She stopped and turned. Those were part of what she'd hoped to get organized and filed away on Saturday, before her day was preempted. "Of course."

"After you get everything figured out in there, could you look through them and give me a list of all the initials you see, along with anything that looks like a dollar amount?"

"You mean like the one we found for EJ?"

Scott's expression was grim. "Yeah. Like that one."

She studied him closely. "If you think those tally sheets had anything to do with Neal's death or with this break-in, we should turn them over to the police."

His grin disarmed her. "I doubt if they do. I'm just curious how much he might have been down, all told. If it's only a few dollars, the police won't care."

Becky certainly didn't think thirty-seven thousand, five hundred would be considered "a few dollars." In her world, twenty dollars at the end of the month seemed like a fortune.

"Sure, I'll do that first thing." She turned back toward the house, Sam at her side.

"Thanks. Oh, and Becky?"

She looked at him over her shoulder.

"Jamie and Tyler are great kids. I had a good time Saturday."

Her heart suddenly light, she returned his smile. "Thanks. We did, too."

Drawing on every ounce of poise she possessed, she headed into the house without looking back. Her step was light enough that the boys would have accused her of skipping. A few seconds later, she heard the heels of his boots striking the driveway as he returned to the barn.

Sam scooted inside when she opened the door, and ran ahead of her through the sitting room. Becky followed, steadfastly ignoring the mess. Scott said he cleaned up in here? The place must have been a disaster. The sofa had been gutted, the side chair was missing and the rack in the corner tilted awkwardly to one side. It was empty, too, which meant she'd have to print more pamphlets.

She thrust that thought away. All in good time. She'd need to clean up the office before worrying about the front room.

As she stepped into the kitchen, music from Scott's radio reached her ears. She smiled, picturing her handsome boss working in the barn.

"He had a good time, Sam." She roughed the yellow fur on the dog's neck, then practically danced over to the corner where his bowls were kept. "He said my boys are great kids."

Sam followed close on her heels, his gaze fixed on her hands as she picked up his water bowl, emptied it and filled it with fresh water for the day. When she set it down, he ignored it. He was more interested in food first thing in the morning.

"Of course, just because he had a good time once doesn't mean anything." She picked up the empty food bowl. Sam's ears perked forward. "A couple of hours at the park with the kids is one thing. An actual date with their mother is entirely different."

That sobering truth dampened her mood and slowed her step as she crossed the kitchen to the pantry, where the giant fifty-five-pound bag of dog food was stored. The door handle was covered in black fingerprint dust, as was every surface in the room. Her lips tightened as she used a paper towel to twist it open. She tugged at the open top of the bag, tilting it toward her so she could scoop out Sam's breakfast.

"We're going to have to add dog food to that list of things Scott said we need, aren't we, Sammy Boy?"

She reached way down into the bag and grabbed the handle of the cup she kept stored inside. When she scooped the cup into the chunks of food, it struck something hard near the bottom.

Odd. She tapped the cup on whatever it was a couple of times, then grasped the edge of the thing. The object was square and solid, but a crinkling sound told her it was wrapped in plastic. She slipped her fingers beneath it and lifted it out.

A plastic sack from the grocery store in town where Neal shopped. Strange. A peek inside told her the block-shaped object was wrapped in a second sack.

The hair on her arms prickled. Neal had buried something in the dog food. Was this what the burglar was after? Or maybe it held a clue as to the identity of his killer. She carried the package over to the kitchen table and set it on the scarred Formica surface. She wouldn't open it, but a quick look couldn't hurt, could it? Peeling away the layers of filmy white plastic, she glimpsed a rectangular object.

Another thick layer of plastic surrounded it, this one secured with wide strips of masking tape. But this plastic was clear.

Becky sank into the seat, her thoughts whirling at the sight of the item in the bag.

A gigantic stack of hundred dollar bills.

# THIRTEEN

"The pantry door was closed, just like always." Becky leaned against the kitchen wall, staring at Detective Foster and Jeff. She tried to resist looking toward the bundle of cash on the table, but her gaze kept straying back to it.

Scott, too, kept glancing that way. It was a huge pile, at least a foot long. They hadn't handled it anymore before the police arrived, but after Jeff unwrapped it, she'd counted twenty-five bundles banded in white paper straps.

"How many bills do you think are in each bundle?" Scott looked at Detective Foster.

"A hundred." The detective answered without hesitation. "That's how they're delivered to the bank from the Federal Reserve."

Becky did a quick calculation. Her eyes went wide as she looked again at the money. If those were all hundred dollar bills, there was two hundred fifty thousand dollars on that table.

"Tell me exactly how you found it." Jeff's pen hovered above the paper, ready to write down her words.

"I was scooping dog food out of the bag, and I felt it in the bottom. I didn't know what it was, so I pulled it out."

She glanced toward Detective Foster, half expecting to

be scolded for tampering with evidence. In retrospect, she should have left it where it was and called the police as soon as she realized something was in there. If she'd known what the bundle contained, she would have.

Foster didn't reprimand her. "How was the package situated in the bag?"

"Exactly like it is now, but wrapped in those two grocery sacks." She nodded toward the discarded sacks beside the money. "It was lengthways, and all the way at the bottom. We're running low on dog food so I was scooping deep."

"How long have you had that bag?" Jeff asked.

Becky closed her eyes, trying to remember. Had Neal bought any dog food since she started working here in February? She didn't think so, but she'd only taken over the job of feeding Sam about a month ago.

She shook her head. "Sorry. It's been here at least a month, but beyond that I have no idea."

They looked at Scott, and he shrugged. "I'm newer than she is."

Jeff glanced at Foster. "Do we need to call the crime lab back?"

Foster pushed the edge of his mustache into his mouth and chewed thoughtfully. Then he shook his head. "They dusted in here yesterday. Whoever burgled the place Saturday night was obviously looking for the money, so if they left any prints we've got them."

Becky caught Scott's eye with a raised eyebrow. Was he going to mention the tally sheets?

He turned to Detective Foster. "Actually, Becky came across something that might be important when she was going through Haldeman's desk on Friday. Apparently the man was a frequent gambler, and we think he might have racked up some fairly significant debt."

Foster and Jeff exchanged a glance. "Like about two hundred fifty thousand dollars' worth?"

Scott shrugged. "We don't know yet. We just found some tally sheets that led me to believe that he's been doing a good deal of betting under the table."

The detective turned to Becky. "Show me."

"They're right in here."

Becky went through the sitting room into the office, the men trailing behind her. She clamped her jaws together at the sight of the mess the burglar had left. Both desks were piled high with a disarray of papers and folders. How could she find anything in this clutter?

She turned to Scott. "Do you remember which desk you put them on?"

He considered, then shook his head. "No, I don't. Sorry."

He went to Haldeman's, and Becky went to her own desk. Together they began sifting through the jumble. She resisted the urge to organize as she went, to put things into piles for filing. Time enough for that later, after the police left.

Foster and Jeff watched in silence as the minutes ticked by. The detective passed the time by chewing on the edge of his mustache.

Scott finished first. "They're not over here."

Becky flipped through the final handful of papers, then shook her head. She raised her head to catch Scott's eye. "Here, either. The thief must have taken them."

"It makes perfect sense." Scott stared into the expressionless face of Detective Foster. "Haldeman had a gambling problem. He hit it big on a bet somewhere and made a boatload of cash. Someone he owed knew about the money and figured he kept it hidden in the barn. The guy broke in, Haldeman heard him, they fought and Haldeman got killed."

The detective's face might as well have been carved from stone. Scott shifted his gaze to Trooper Whitley. "It even explains why Sam was confined in the house that night. Haldeman left him here to guard the real location of the cash while he investigated the barn."

Beside him, Becky nodded. "That does make a lot of sense."

Whitley looked skeptical, but at least he had showed some expression. "So where did he get the cash?"

"From one of his bookies, probably." Scott hooked his thumb through a belt loop. "There are always races to bet on, and a confirmed gambler likes the big odds. Occasionally, one is bound to pay off. Maybe after the bookie turned over the money, he decided to come back for it. If we can find the guy who paid Haldeman that money, we might just find the killer."

"It does make sense," said Whitley.

Scott nodded. Now they were getting somewhere. "Haldeman recorded the initials of the bookie he placed each bet with on those tally sheets. We were going to compile a list of them today." He waved at the mess. "Still, it shouldn't be too hard to find out who Haldeman did business with." He crossed the floor and stopped in front of Detective Foster. "So what's our next step? Interrogate the bookies?"

The detective's expression took on the texture of granite. He awarded Scott a chilly smile. "Thank you for your opinions, Mr. Lewis. We'll keep them in mind. But for obvious reasons we can't discuss our investigation with you in any detail. And I must advise you against doing any investigative work on your own. Leave that to the experts."

Scott shoved a hand in his pocket. He felt like he'd been slapped down. They weren't even going to talk to him about it, and after he'd turned over all the physical evidence he'd uncovered. He was just trying to cooperate, and he really could help. He had connections.

But they probably had more connections than he did. They didn't need his help. He should just focus on the horses, do his job and let the cops do theirs.

Still, they didn't have to be so condescending.

"I understand." He clipped the words short.

"So, is that it?" Detective Foster's gaze swept from Scott to Becky.

Becky shrugged. "That's all we know."

Whitley clicked his pen and closed his notebook with a snap. "You'll let us know if you discover anything else missing?"

Scott unclamped his mouth long enough to answer. "You bet."

Whitley's lips twitched. "Pun intended?"

Ha, ha. Scott rolled his eyes, and the officer turned away chuckling. Becky followed them to the back door, but Scott stayed where he was, staring at the piles of junk everywhere. Whoever broke in here wasn't concerned with hiding his or her tracks. If it had been him, he would have searched for the money carefully and tried not to leave a trace that he'd been here.

The storm door slammed, and moments later Becky returned to the room. "You didn't tell them about EJ." Her voice held a touch of accusation.

Scott lifted a shoulder. "They didn't ask."

"They didn't know to ask."

"Hey!" He held out his hands, fingers splayed. "We told them about the initials. You can bet they know every bookie in the state. They'll probably have a list of Haldeman's buddies by the end of the day, which is more than we'll have."

She folded her arms across her chest. "Why do I get the feeling you're planning to make your own list?"

"Well, I do have a few contacts. Won't hurt to ask a question or two." His glance slid away from her shrewd stare. He hadn't mentioned his conversation with Eddie Jones, and didn't see any reason to now. "If I discover anything important I'll turn it over to them."

"Mmm, hmm."

He fought the impulse to squirm under her stare. Which was ridiculous. He wasn't doing anything wrong, just following up on a hunch that Detective Foster obviously didn't think had merit. It wasn't like he was doing a real investigation or anything. He was just going to talk to a friend. He returned her stare.

She turned away quickly, but not before he saw a flash of emotion in her eyes. Concern, maybe?

"Do me a favor, would you, Scott?" She busied herself with shuffling papers into a neat stack as she spoke. "Be careful. I've lost one boss already."

Her head was lowered over her desk so he could only see the top of her head, but there was no mistaking her tone. She was worried about him. Warmth flooded his gut. It had been a long time since a woman felt protective enough about him to worry.

He made a snap decision. "Listen, I was wondering if you ever have any free time? You know, without the kids. Like maybe for dinner or something?"

She looked up, her wide eyes searching his face. A smile tugged at the corners of her mouth.

"It has been a long time," she admitted.

"How about tomorrow, then?"

"On a school night?"

He didn't even think about that. He fiddled with a paper clip on the surface of the desk. "Oh. Yeah. Sorry. I forgot."

"It's okay. I can probably manage to find a babysitter, as long as we don't stay out too late."

The thin metal rod of the clip jabbed into his finger as he straightened it. He dropped it on the desk and shoved his hand into his pocket. "So I'll pick you up at seven?"

The smile broke free, igniting her eyes. "That sounds good."

He couldn't believe he was doing this. He hadn't been on a date in years. He stood rooted to the floor, staring into her face until a pretty blush stained her cheeks and she looked away.

"Great." He turned toward Haldeman's desk, changed his mind, and swiveled to march toward the door. "I'll get directions to your house later."

Sam leaped off the cushionless couch to follow him as he escaped to the barn.

# FOURTEEN

Scott paced down the center aisle of the horse barn, nodding at a pair of guys mucking a stall on his right. They were working late today. The stable boys usually tore out of here at four o'clock, and it was almost five now. At the far end of the barn, he tapped on the glass window of the door to the Shady Acres Farm office, then cracked it open.

"Zach, can I chew your ear for a minute?"

His former boss looked up from the desk, and a smile brightened his craggy face. "Sure thing. Come on in."

Scott sat in the seat across the old wooden desk's scratched surface. The room felt stuffy, thanks to the space heater Zach always ran when he was pushing papers. The gruff farm manager said he could take any amount of cold as long as he was doing something physical, but his fifty-five-year-old joints stiffened up if he sat still too long.

Zach rocked back in his desk chair, work-roughened hands folded across his stomach. "How's it going over there at the Pasture? You handling everything? You know you can call me if you need any help with those stallions."

"Thanks, but it's going great." Scott crossed his legs and rested his forearm on his knee. "Except we had some more excitement this morning."

He filled Zach in on the robbery, and Becky's big find of the day. As he spoke, the older man's jaw inched open until it gaped.

"You gotta be kidding me. Two hundred fifty *thousand* dollars? In a bag of dog food?" He gave a low whistle. "Do the cops think the guy who killed Haldeman was after the money?"

A grunt of disgust escaped Scott's lips. "Who knows what they think. But it fits, you know?"

Zach nodded, his thick gray eyebrows high. "It sure is a lot of money. Men have been killed for less."

"We found something else the other day. Apparently, Haldeman was into Eddie Jones for a fairly significant chunk of change. And Jones wasn't the only one Haldeman owed."

"I'm not surprised. He liked to play the ponies, no doubt about it." Zach speared him with a gaze. "You don't think Jones killed him, do you?"

"I don't know." Scott kept his face impassive. "But I did have a talk with him Friday afternoon out at Keeneland, and I mentioned finding his name in Haldeman's records. And guess what's missing after the break-in?"

Zach steepled his fingers and tapped them in front of his face as he studied Scott through narrowed eyes. He shook his head. "I don't peg Jones as a killer, but he'd eat a load of manure for that kind of cash. And if Haldeman caught him snooping around the place, and they got into a fight?"

Scott sat against the hard chair back. "That's what I thought, too. And if it wasn't Jones, it could have been someone else. Unfortunately, I don't know who Haldeman did business with." He caught Zach's eye. "Do you?"

A slow smile spread across the older man's face. "Now

why would you think I'd have any idea about something like that?"

Scott returned his grin. "Just a wild guess."

He chuckled. "Well, I have been known to place a wager every now and then." His hands dropped to the desk, and his expression sobered. "But I never talked to Haldeman about it. He might have used Edwards, or Kavanaugh, or maybe McMatthews. Jones would know."

"He would?"

Zach nodded. "They always know who else their customers are playing with, especially if the numbers start getting big. Makes sense, if you think about it."

It did. A smart businessman knew the total debt level of his customers. Especially a customer whose tab was growing.

Of course, Eddie had no reason to share that information with Scott. But it couldn't hurt to ask, could it? They didn't have a chance to finish their conversation at the race track the other day after Kaci interrupted them.

"I guess I'll have to pay Eddie another visit." Scott got to his feet. He might be able to catch him at the track. Oh. Today was Monday. No racing at Keeneland on Mondays.

"You don't happen to know where I can find him, do you?"

Zach glanced at his watch. "He'll be down at O'Grady's in another half hour."

O'Grady's was a sports bar in downtown Lexington. Scott had heard of it, but since he didn't make a practice of hanging out in bars of any kind, he'd never been there.

Zach put his hands on the edge of the desk and rolled his chair backward. "You want me to go with you? I got a thing tonight, but I can cancel it."

"Thanks, but that's not necessary."

Zach paused in the act of standing. "You sure about that?"

A rush of gratitude washed over Scott. "I'm sure."

The older man lowered himself back into the chair. He rolled up to the desk and caught Scott's gaze. "Be careful, son. Some of these guys don't take kindly to questions."

Scott nodded and slipped through the door quickly so the heat didn't escape. As he walked between rows of clean stalls, his step felt light. Zach could be crotchety, and the stable hands trod lightly around him, but when push came to shove, he was a loyal friend. The second person today to exhibit real concern for Scott's safety. It was enough to make a man stop and count his blessings.

"Please, Amber. The boys would be so excited."

Becky hated begging, but she was desperate. She propped the phone with a shoulder and pressed a sticky label on a file as she waited for her friend's response.

"I don't know." Amber's voice held so much reluctance Becky could almost see the scowl on her face. "I don't have any babysitting experience, you know."

"You don't need experience." Becky glanced at the wall clock. Four fifty-eight. Close enough. She crossed the room and locked the front door, phone still pressed to her ear. "You like kids, don't you?"

"Selectively." Becky chuckled at her dry tone. "Let me be honest with you," Amber went on. "Your boys scare me! They're rowdy and loud, and yesterday at church I saw one of them sucker punch the other for no reason at all."

Becky cringed. Tyler. She tried to keep the pleading out of her voice. "They would be on their best behavior with you. They love you."

"Why can't you just hire a teenager?"

"The truth?" She sat on the edge of the desk. "I can't afford a teenager. I figured you'd let me take you out to lunch after church one Sunday as payment."

"I don't know, Becky."

Amber still didn't sound convinced. Frustrated, Becky tapped her toe on the carpet. She did have a Plan B, though it came with far more strings than she liked. "I guess I could call Pastor Vaughn and Donna. They might watch the boys for me, if I beg them."

"You are desperate if you're willing to subject yourself and your love life to Donna's questions." A resigned sigh blew through the phone. "Okay, I'll do it."

Grinning, Becky hopped off the desk. "Thank you so much. I owe you big-time."

"Yes, you do. And lunch won't take care of this debt. I'm going to hold it over your head for a while until I figure out an appropriate payment."

"Anything. I promise. You are the best friend a girl can have."

"Yeah, yeah. I'll see you tomorrow a little before seven."

Becky dropped the phone into its cradle and almost skipped around the desk to get her purse from the bottom door. She had a date! Just wait until she told Daddy.

As she slammed the drawer shut, the phone rang again. She hesitated. The office officially closed at five.

She snatched it up. "Out to Pasture."

"My, my, my. If it isn't the little *secretary*."

No mistaking that voice. She'd recognize that fake drawl anywhere. "Hello, Miss Buchanan. What can I do for you?"

"You?" A haughty laugh sounded. "Not a thing. I'm calling for Scott."

The comment set Becky's teeth on edge, but she kept

her voice professionally polite. "He's not here. May I leave him a message?"

"I don't *think* so." She paused. "On second thought, yes. Tell him how much I enjoyed seeing him the other evening, and that I can't wait for the next time."

A hot flush dampened Becky's neck. Scott was with Kaci recently? Since she'd been here when Kaci made her appearance Friday morning, and Kaci said *evening,* she must be referring to a different time. A date, maybe? A sick knot formed in Becky's stomach.

"Did you get that down, or do I need to speak slower?"

The knot exploded into anger at the insult.

"I got it. You can't wait for the next time." Becky snapped the words. A catty comment shot from her mouth before she could stop it. "Should I ask him to check his couch for your other earring?"

"Oooh, the pony has a kick." Kaci's voice lowered, but lost none of its stinging conceit. "By the way, little pony, I don't appreciate having the police show up at my home unannounced, asking awkward questions. It makes for an uncomfortable evening."

A few uncomfortable evenings wouldn't hurt the haughty woman, in Becky's opinion. But her hackles were standing at full attention now, and she found herself wanting to punch back. "The police asked us to keep them informed. And even you must admit, having a prominent person stoop to such a blatant trick to get a man's attention is a little bit suspicious." She rushed on, anger causing blood to roar in her ears. "It must have hurt your pride to have Neal's attention directed some-where else."

Her laugh was genuine. "Trust me, darling, that filly

isn't in the same class as me, on the track or off. She's an upstart, that's what she is. Neal was only dallying with her."

Fierce loyalty rose up in Becky "You're right. She's not in the same class. Isabelle Keller's got more class in her little finger than—"

"Isabelle? Neal was involved with Isabelle?"

The surprise in Kaci's voice dumped icy water on Becky's anger. If she didn't know about Isabelle, then who was Kaci talking about?

"Uh, well, I…" Becky stammered her way into silence. She couldn't very well say anything else without betraying Isabelle's confidence.

Thank goodness Kaci didn't push for details. "He was a busy man, wasn't he? Not surprising, though. Neal knew how to treat a woman. If he chose to spread his charm widely, who cares?" Her voice hardened. "But my earring was a private concern, and of no interest to the police."

"If you've done nothing wrong, then you've got nothing to worry about."

"Oh, I am not worried. Merely annoyed." She paused. "Given your social standing, perhaps you aren't aware of the risks involved in annoying a Buchanan."

Becky's heart thump-thumped. "Are you threatening me?"

Kaci laughed. "A warning only, darling. Keep in mind that ponies can't run with Thoroughbreds in *any* race. They just don't stand a chance."

A click sounded in Becky's ear. She stood in place, the dead phone in her hand. There wasn't a single doubt in her mind what Kaci's warning was about. Scott.

She replaced the receiver and picked up her purse. Her

spirits, so high a few minutes before, now hovered somewhere in the vicinity of her shoes.

How could she compete with someone like Kaci Buchanan?

O'Grady's was a hopping place on Monday nights. Scott found a parking place on the street and walked three blocks to the busy little bar. The patrons spilled out onto the sidewalk in front of the building, many of them puffing on cigarettes they couldn't take inside.

Scott held his breath as he made his way through a cloud of smoke and into the bar. As the door closed behind him, he stepped to one side to let his eyes adjust to the dim light. The pungent odors of beer and bourbon prickled his nostrils.

A polished bar ran the length of the long room on the left, and when he could see he recognized a few of the people perched on stools there. A row of tables lined the opposite wall, each with four chairs and most of them full. Television sets hung suspended from the ceiling throughout the place. A loud shout went up from two of the tables to his right, and several men jumped to their feet, fists thrust into the air.

He spotted Eddie at the far end of the bar, his head bowed as he listened to the man next to him. A customer, probably. The man's hands moved constantly as he spoke, and occasionally Eddie nodded.

Scott made his way to the empty stool beside Eddie's customer and slid onto the seat. The man, whose back was turned toward Scott, kept talking, but Eddie looked up. Their eyes locked.

Scott had the sense Eddie was not surprised to see him tonight.

"What'll you have?" The muscled bartender swiped a damp towel across the bar in front of Scott.

Asking for iced tea in this place probably wasn't a good idea. He might get more than he bargained for. "A Coke's fine."

The guy's expression didn't change. He tossed a cocktail napkin onto the bar and turned away to get Scott's Coke. Scott watched as he scooped ice into a glass, then poured soda from a hose. Beside him, the man's voice droned on, low enough that Scott could only make out a word here and there.

"…seventh…carry me…handle another fifty…"

"I can do that." Because Eddie faced him, his voice carried to Scott's ears clearly. "Just make sure you're here on the seventh."

The man got off the stool, uttering profuse thanks, as the bartender returned with Scott's Coke. With a nod in his direction, Scott slid his glass, napkin and all, across the bar in front of the vacated stool.

"Mind if I sit here?" He moved onto the stool without waiting for an answer.

Eddie cocked his head. "It's a public place."

"I was hoping we could continue our conversation."

Eddie picked up a thin straw and folded it with a finger and a thumb. "I thought we finished the other day."

"Ah, but more has happened since then."

A smile flashed onto his narrow face, gone as quickly as it appeared. "I heard you had some excitement out at the Pasture. Something about a robbery?"

Scott studied him. Was the man mocking him? Hard to tell with that sardonic expression. "I figured you might know something about it."

Eddie picked up his glass, which had a sliver of lime perched on the side, and sipped. "I don't know anything more than I read in the paper this morning. Apparently the thief got away with about fifty bucks?" His shoulders jerked with a silent laugh.

He was mocking him. Scott was sure of it. He kept a tight rein on his temper. He was here to get information from the guy, not antagonize him. "And a couple of other things, as well. But he didn't find the real stash. I did."

Eddie's expression remained unchanged. He sipped from his glass again, then set it on the bar. "Here's where I'm supposed to ask what you found."

"Two hundred fifty thousand dollars in cash."

If Scott hadn't been watching him closely he would have missed the flicker of surprise, the quick movement of his eyes.

"That's a lot of money. Too bad Haldeman didn't use it to pay his debts before he cashed in his chips."

What a callous attitude. An intense dislike for the man in front of him came over Scott. Here was someone who made a living from other people's weaknesses. He didn't care for his clients one bit, that was obvious. "Yeah, it might have saved his life if he had."

The man straightened as he turned on his stool so that he faced Scott directly. Angry white lines creased the skin around his tightened lips. "I don't like what I think I hear you saying."

Scott stiffened his spine, too. He'd tried hard to keep the accusation out of his voice. Apparently he failed. "All I'm saying is on Friday I told you Haldeman had records mentioning your name, and Saturday night they were stolen. A day later a wad of cash turns up. Now those things might be coincidence, but when you add them to the fact that

# A SERIES OF EDGE-OF-YOUR-SEAT SUSPENSE NOVELS!

# GET 2 FREE BOOKS!

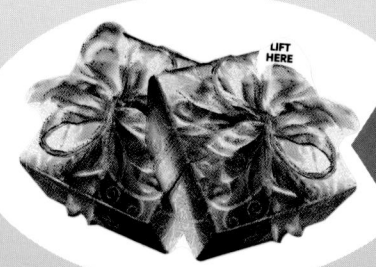

LIFT HERE

To get your 2 free books, affix this peel-off sticker to the reply card and mail it today!

*Plus, receive*

# TWO FREE BONUS GIFTS!

## Love Inspired® SUSPENSE

RIVETING INSPIRATIONAL ROMANCE

**W**e'd like to send you two free books to introduce you to the Love Inspired® Suspense series. Your two books have a combined c[...] price of $9.98 in the U.S. and $11.98 in Canada, but they are yours [...] We'll even send you two wonderful surprise gifts. You can't lose!

Each of your **FREE** books is filled with riveting inspirational suspense featuring Christian characters facing challenges to t[...] faith...and their lives!

# GET 2 FREE BOOKS!

## HURRY!
**Return this card promptly to get 2 FREE Books and 2 FREE Bonus Gifts!**

**YES!** Please send me the **2 FREE Love Inspired® Suspense books** and **2 FREE gifts** for which I qualify. I understand that I am under no obligation to purchase anything further, as explained on the back of this card.

*Love Inspired*
## SUSPENSE
RIVETING INSPIRATIONAL ROMANCE

**PLACE FREE GIFTS SEAL HERE**

323 IDL EL5D          123 IDL EL4D

| | |
|---|---|
| FIRST NAME | LAST NAME |

ADDRESS

| | |
|---|---|
| APT.# | CITY |

| | |
|---|---|
| STATE/PROV. | ZIP/POSTAL CODE |

◀ DETACH AND MAIL CARD TODAY!

LISUS-IV-07

Haldeman was killed in that same place just a few days before, it starts to stink."

Fury shone in Eddie's eyes as he slipped off the stool to glare down at Scott from his full towering height. "The only stink I smell around here is you and your insinuations."

"Is there a problem, gentlemen?"

Scott looked away from the fury in Eddie's face. The bartender, hamlike hands on the surface of the bar as he bent across it, slid a menacing stare from Scott to Eddie. Around them, all conversations had ceased as the nearby patrons watched openly.

Okay, not a good idea to continue this. Besides, he wouldn't get a list of Haldeman's other bookies from Eddie now. Nor did he need to. He'd come in here looking for information, but he might have gotten more than he bargained for. If Scott's hunch could be trusted, he was staring at the man responsible for Haldeman's death.

He stood. "No problem. I was just leaving."

He pulled a few dollars out of his pocket and threw them next to his untouched drink. With one more look into Eddie Jones's furious face, he turned and walked to the door, aware that dozens of eyes watched him go.

# FIFTEEN

Becky stood inside the back door staring across the Pasture's paddocks. When she arrived for work an hour ago, Scott was already out on the cart doing his morning chores. Looked as though he'd just finished with Dark Diego in the farthest pasture.

She bit back a yawn and resisted the impulse to rub her tired eyes. Sleep had proven elusive most of the night. Instead, she replayed her conversation with Kaci over and over. By the time she finally dozed off, she'd come to the conclusion that the footprints in the barn probably didn't belong to the snooty Kaci. Nor did she believe they belonged to Isabelle. But Kaci evidently knew the identity of a third woman, probably the same one who signed the note they found "L."

Outside, Scott turned the cart around and headed toward the barn. Becky stepped back from the door. Hopefully he didn't see her watching. She returned to her desk and her task of refiling the last of the documents the thief had dumped on the floor.

Of course, she could simply call Kaci and ask her the woman's name. But subjecting herself to another conversation with that conceited snob wasn't an appealing thought. No, much better to let the police handle things.

Becky fought against an uncharitable smile at the thought of the police paying a second visit to Miss Kaci Buchanan. With her compliments.

"Good morning." Scott's voice preceded the banging of the back door. His footsteps went into the kitchen, followed by the sound of water running.

"Hello," she answered. "How was your evening?"

He stepped through the doorway, gulping from a glass. "Interesting." His gaze fell to her clean desk. "Hey, you've about got it whipped."

"I do. And I'm proud to say the files are in better shape now than they were before." She picked up the sticky note on the center of her desk and kept her expression impassive as she held her index finger toward him, the yellow square stuck on the end. "You've got a message."

He crossed the room with three long strides to pluck the note off her finger. Becky straightened the position of the pad and placed the pen beside it, trying not to watch as he read.

"Hmm." A puzzled frown drew lines on his forehead. Then it cleared as he folded the paper and shoved it in his pocket. "Oh, I forgot to tell you to add a bottle of Hoof Heal to the list of supplies from Simpson's. Have you already placed the order?"

Unspoken questions burned on Becky's tongue, but she managed to control herself. "Yes, but they haven't delivered yet." She reached for the phone. "There's probably time—"

"Is anyone here?"

Becky identified the voice calling from the back door at the same moment its owner stepped into the office. Detective Foster, followed by Jeff. Good. Their presence would save her a phone call to tell them about the third woman. She bit back a greeting when she saw their solemn expressions.

Scott must have noted the same, because his tone was guarded. "What can we do for you this morning?"

Foster's eyes flicked to her before settling on Scott's face. "For starters, you can tell me where you were around one o'clock this morning."

Scott's spine stiffened. "Why do you want to know?"

"Would you answer the question, please?"

Why was the detective acting so politely hostile? Becky caught Jeff's gaze and raised an eyebrow. He gave a very slight shake of his head, then stared pointedly at Scott.

Scott's shoulders rose as he pocketed both hands. "I was in bed."

"Alone?"

"Of course alone." A smile flashed onto his lips. "Sam slept on the couch."

Foster's expression did not change. "What time did you get home, Mr. Lewis?"

"Around nine, I'd say. I spent some extra time with Thunder last night because his hooves needed attention."

"And before that? Did you go anywhere at all last evening?"

Scott's eyelids narrowed. "Actually, yes, I did. But I get the impression you already know that."

The detective dipped his forehead, conceding the point. "We have statements from several witnesses who said you were at O'Grady's Tavern in Lexington last night around six o'clock."

Becky looked quickly at Scott. She didn't think he was the kind of guy who frequented bars. Church, yes. But a bar? She shifted in her chair, suddenly uncomfortable.

He nodded, his lips tight.

Foster continued. "And that you had a conversation with an Edward Jones?"

Becky's eyes widened as the name registered. That had to be the EJ from Neal's betting records. Relief washed over her. Scott just went to the bar to talk to Neal's bookie. Thank goodness. She'd had enough of men who thought a bar was a great place to hang out.

"You want to tell me what all this is about, Detective?" The stubborn set of Scott's jaw must have told the detective he wasn't going to answer any more questions blindly.

Foster nodded toward Jeff, his gaze never leaving Scott's face.

The trooper stepped forward. "Mr. Edward Jones was murdered in his home around one this morning. The killer broke through a rear window and surprised him in bed."

A loud gasp escaped Becky's open mouth. Another murder?

Surely no one could mistake the shock on Scott's face. His chin dropped as he stumbled backward to sit heavily on the surface of the other desk. He opened his mouth, closed it, swallowed hard, and then managed to choke out, "How?"

"We thought you might tell us."

Becky cringed at the accusation in Detective Foster's tone.

Scott's eyes went wide. "You can't think I killed Eddie Jones?"

Jeff answered. "The witnesses who place you at the bar also say you and Mr. Jones argued, and that you left in a hurry."

"That's right. I left because he got hostile, and the bartender was about to throw us both out."

"Why did he 'get hostile'?"

Scott's chest rose as he drew a deep breath. "Because I accused him of breaking into the Pasture's office, and insinuated that he had something to do with Haldeman's death."

Detective Foster closed his eyes and shook his head. "Mr. Lewis, I warned you not to try to investigate this case on your own."

"If you suspected Edward Jones of anything, you should have told us instead of trying to talk to the guy yourself." Jeff's voice was hard.

"Okay, yeah. In retrospect, that would have been the smart thing to do."

He sounded so defeated that Becky tried to infuse as much confidence in her smile as she could when he glanced her way. His lips curved upward in response.

Then he folded his arms and asked, "Am I being arrested?"

Becky sat forward on the edge of her chair, waiting for the answer. Surely no one could seriously suspect Scott of such a monstrous act. When Detective Foster didn't immediately deny it, she threw a panicked look toward Jeff, but he refused to meet her eye.

The silence stretched uncomfortably before Foster finally answered. "Not at this time. But we need to get your statement. And until further notice, it would be unwise to leave town without letting one of us know." Scott stared at the floor, his lips tight. "We'd also like to take a look at your truck and your home."

His head jerked up. Detective Foster returned his glare with equanimity.

Finally, Scott gave a single nod. "Go ahead. I have nothing to hide."

Jeff stepped toward the door. "If you'll come with me, then."

Scott followed him out of the house. As Detective Foster turned to leave, Becky rose from her chair.

"Detective, I have something I need to tell you."

He turned a polite expression her way.

When she heard the back door close behind Scott and Jeff, she cleared her throat. "It concerns that note you and Trooper Whitley found. I have a feeling Kaci Buchanan knows who L is."

His eyebrows arched. "What makes you think so?"

Becky repeated their conversation, leaving out the parts about Isabelle and Scott. "So she obviously knows Neal was involved with another woman."

He pressed the corner of his mustache into his mouth as he studied her for a moment. Finally, he spoke. "Mrs. Dennison, we've already disturbed Miss Buchanan once. She was entirely forthcoming, and we specifically asked if she knew of anyone else who might have visited Mr. Haldeman's barn. She denied any such knowledge."

"Then she lied." Becky raised her chin. "Something I have no doubt she can do with a great deal of skill."

A real smile curved Foster's mouth. He spoke gently. "Perhaps it was not me she lied to."

Becky felt a flush creep up her neck. "Why would she lie to me?"

"Perhaps to upset you?"

He stared at her until she looked away. She had to admit the possibility that Kaci would lie just to mess with her.

"That's possible," she conceded. "But I don't think so. She sounded too surprised when I—" She snapped her mouth shut.

"Yes?"

Becky chewed on the inside of her lip. She hadn't

planned to say anything about Isabelle. But under his piercing stare, she couldn't hold back.

She stared at the floor between them. "We were discussing another of Neal's girlfriends, Isabelle Keller."

"The daughter of Hugh Keller." His voice was flat.

She nodded. "Kaci didn't know about her, and obviously thought I was talking about this third woman. When I mentioned Isabelle's name, she was surprised." She looked up. "So that's why I don't think she was lying. Not to me, anyway."

He studied her a moment longer, then gave a single nod. "If we have reason to question Miss Buchanan further, I will certainly ask her to verify her previous statement about not knowing any other women who had opportunity to visit the barn here."

What did *if we have reason* mean? "You mean you're not going to—"

"Thank you, Mrs. Dennison. And now, I will stress to you the same thing I told Mr. Lewis yesterday. Do not attempt any further investigation on your own. Leave it to the professionals."

Feeling as though her hands had been slapped, Becky managed a sulky nod.

# SIXTEEN

"After they searched Scott's truck, they took him over to his house and searched there, too. But they didn't find anything, of course."

Becky kept her voice low, glancing down the hallway toward the boys' bedroom.

"Jeff never mentioned a thing." Amber scowled. "But he never talks about his cases until they're over. Police rules or something." She winced as a crash echoed down the hallway, and threw an anxious glance at Becky.

Becky flashed an apologetic grimace as she trotted toward the boys' bedroom.

"All right, misters, stop it this instant!"

Entangled like a pretzel on the floor, they froze. Identical looks of surprise turned her way. Both were playing a less-than-friendly game of tug-of-war with a yellow dump truck.

Becky spoke in her sternest voice. "If you don't want to spend the whole week in time-out, you had better behave yourselves tonight. Aunt Amber is doing Mommy a favor, and I don't want you to make her sorry she did."

Tyler scowled and released the truck to fold his arms across his chest. "I don't know why we can't come, too."

A quick reply came to mind, but Becky stopped herself. Was this the jealousy Daddy told her might occur? She'd dated only a couple of times since her divorce, and the last time had been over a year ago when they were four. They were older now, closer to the age when they might really resent a man claiming their mother's attention.

She dropped to her knees, careful to avoid the assortment of cars and connecting blocks scattered around the floor. "You can't go because Mr. Lewis and I want to spend some time alone so we can get to know each other better. You'll have fun here with Aunt Amber."

Jamie spun a wheel on the upturned dump truck. "He could get to know me and Tyler, too."

"I'm sure he'd like that another time. Besides, we're going to a fancy restaurant where there won't be any other kids and you can't make any noise. You'd get really bored."

Tyler scowled. "Then why do you want to go?"

She laughed and ruffled his hair. "Because they have cool things to eat, like snails."

"Eeewww, yucky!"

Both boys rolled on the floor, clutching their stomachs and making gagging noises. When she tickled their tummies, the gagging turned to giggles.

After as much roughhousing as Becky could comfortably handle in a skirt and panty hose, she got to her feet.

"Mommy?"

Tyler looked up at her, his expression serious, dark eyes full of concern. Was this it? Was this where they'd ask her if she still loved them even if she liked Mr. Lewis?

Her heart twisted as she looked down into the beloved little face. "Yes, sweetheart?"

"Sam's not going is he? 'Cause if Sam goes, I get to go, too."

Jamie leaped to his feet. "Me, too. I want to go with Sam."

She kept the laughter out of her expression. "No, Sam is not going."

"Okay." Their concerns resolved, they returned to their task of picking out the perfect toy to show Aunt Amber.

Becky went back to the living room, chuckling.

The doorbell rang. Two tornadoes sped past her, each shouting, "I'll get it!"

They opened the door before Becky could stop them. When she caught sight of Scott on the front stoop, her protest died on her lips. She'd never seen him in anything but jeans. Tonight he wore dark tailored pants, a gray dress shirt and a sport coat. His model-like good looks made her mouth dry. This gorgeous guy was here for *her* when he could have someone as beautiful as Kaci Buchanan? What did she do to deserve this?

"Hey, guys, how's it going?" Scott's smile widened when he looked up at her. "Hello. You look fantastic."

*Be still my heart.* "Thanks."

His gaze swept the room, and she allowed hers to follow, seeing her cramped home with fresh eyes. The furniture was nearly as shabby as the Pasture's before it got ripped to shreds. And what was that smell? Why had she cooked fish sticks for the boys' supper tonight, of all nights? Heat flooded her face, and she grabbed Amber's arm to pull her forward. "Scott, I'd like you to meet my friend, Amber Craig. Jeff Whitley is her boyfriend."

Scott's smile was nothing but polite as he shook her hand. In return, Amber examined him with a friendly but curious gaze.

"I've heard a lot about you, Scott." Her eyes widened and she glanced quickly at Becky. "Uh, I mean from Becky. Not from Jeff. He would never talk about a suspect. Uh, not that Becky said—I mean, she told me…" She winced and lowered her eyes. Becky cringed. So much for making a good impression.

Thank goodness for kids who forgot their manners. They interrupted what might have become an awkward moment by tugging on Scott's arms.

"Come see our toys, Mr. Lewis," Tyler urged.

"Sorry, boys, we need to get going." Becky glanced pointedly at her watch, then at Amber. "Do you have any questions before we leave?"

Amber's face had gone from red to white at Becky's announcement. "About a million. What do they eat? When is bedtime? Do they go to the bathroom alone?" She wore a please-don't-leave-me-alone-with-them expression that made Becky chuckle.

"They've already eaten, eight-thirty, and yes." She gathered the panicky woman in a quick hug. "Don't worry. You'll be fine."

Becky pressed a quick kiss onto each of the boys' cheeks and slipped outside after Scott. When the door closed behind her, she leaned against it and wiped an imaginary bead of sweat off her forehead.

Scott laughed. "I take it this is her first babysitting job."

"Yes, and she had to be coerced into it." She cast an anxious glance over her shoulder. "I hope she'll be okay."

"Don't worry, Mother Goose." He placed a hand at her back and propelled her toward his truck. "She looks like she can handle your little goslings."

"Hey!" Becky pulled away from his touch and whirled

to walk backward so she could look at him. "I don't want to be Mother Goose tonight. I want to be Cinderella, going to the ball." She reached the truck and leaned against it, tilting her head to cast a flirtatious grin up at him.

Admiration lit his eyes. "I'll be Prince Charming to your Cinderella any day."

He leaned toward her, and butterflies took flight in Becky's stomach. But instead of kissing her, he grabbed the door handle and opened it for her.

When she had stepped up into the truck and slid onto the bench seat, he placed an arm on the back and bent forward to capture her eyes in an intense gaze. "I have only one request for the evening."

She would have promised him anything if only he would go on looking at her like that. "What is it?"

He grinned. "Let's not talk about the Pasture, or Haldeman, or murder suspects, or anything related to any of the above."

On that, they were in wholehearted agreement.

At ten-twenty, Becky closed the living room door behind her and sank against it with a rapturous sigh.

"Welcome home," whispered Amber from the couch. "Did you have fun?"

"Oh, Amber!" She closed her eyes and let a dreamy smile take her lips. "It was the most wonderful evening I've ever had. He is handsome and kind and smart and considerate. And a strong Christian! I think he knows the Bible as well as Pastor Vaughn." She grinned triumphantly. "We'll see tomorrow, because he's coming here for dinner and then to church with us!"

"I'm glad you had a nice time." Amber sounded tired.

As her friend struggled to her feet, Becky looked around the room. "What happened in here?"

The place was a disaster. Toys were strewn everywhere, the curtains dangled off the rod at one end and a brown handprint had been smeared across the television screen. Jamie was curled up in a slumbering ball on the floor, while Tyler had collapsed across the coffee table, his feet still on the floor. Drool puddled beneath his open mouth on the table's surface.

"I made a critical mistake." Amber's lips twisted at her blunder. "I tried to bribe them into being good with chocolate."

Becky's hand flew to her mouth. "Oh, no."

Scowling, Amber nodded. "They were wound tighter than a couple of springs."

A hint of concern crept into Becky's voice as she stepped farther into the room to examine her friend. She looked as if she'd been mugged. "What is that gunk in your hair?"

"Peanut butter." She tried to wipe off a blob of goo with her fingers and managed to rub it in even more. "One of them, I have no idea which, came up with the great idea of slathering the chocolate bars with peanut butter."

"Oh, Amber, I'm so sorry. They're usually—" She stopped. She was about to say the boys were well-behaved if you were firm with them, but the look on her friend's face warned her now was not the time to share child-raising tips.

"Yeah, whatever."

Becky winced at Amber's caustic tone. She bent to pick up a candy wrapper, then started to lay a hand on Tyler's back to rouse him and send him to bed.

"Don't!"

Amber's loud hiss made her jerk her hand back. "Don't what?"

"Don't wake them until I'm gone." She dashed into the kitchen and returned in a second, purse clutched in her hand and a frantic expression on her face. "Just give me a thirty-second head start. Good night. See you at church."

She ran from the house without a backward glance. The slam of the door shook the dangling curtain rod off the wall.

# SEVENTEEN

"Samson's Secret is one of the friendliest horses we have here at the Pasture." Scott slapped the old bay's neck affectionately as six tourists gathered around him. "He was found abandoned in a field in New Jersey, nothing but a bag of bones living on rainwater and whatever wild grass he could find. The authorities checked his tattoo and realized who he was, a champion who had made more than a million dollars during his career. He still holds the six-furlong track record at Arlington." Scott shook his head. "It was like finding Babe Ruth living under a bridge."

"He's a beautiful horse." The woman reached a tentative hand toward Samson, smiling when he allowed her to rub his nose.

"Here, give him this." Scott pulled an apple out of the bucket he carried and halved it with his pocket knife.

She did, turning a wide grin on her husband when Samson took it eagerly from her fingers.

Scott laughed. "Besides being the friendliest, he's the best eater. Probably remembers what it was like to scavenge for food."

"What's wrong with his ear?" One of the men pointed.

Scott stepped closer to the fence to grasp Samson's halter.

The edge of his ear had a cut, fairly fresh. It looked clean, but he should probably put some antibiotic ointment on it to keep it from getting infected. Have to remember to do that.

He looked at the man and shrugged. "They get little nicks and cuts every so often, especially the ones who like to roll on the ground or rub against the fence."

His cell phone buzzed on his belt. He unclipped it and glanced at the number. Lee Courtney.

"Excuse me a minute." He nodded toward his audience before stepping a few feet away. They drew together in a tight cluster around Samson, who appeared to be enjoying all the attention.

"Scott Lewis."

"Scott, this is Marion. Lee would like to see you this afternoon, if you have time."

Scott wanted to get his evening chores done early so he could relax and enjoy Becky's church. But of course he'd make time for his boss. "You bet. What time?"

He heard a paper shuffle, then Lee's assistant said, "He's free around four. Just come on up to the house."

"I'll be there." Hopefully the meeting wouldn't take too long. He was supposed to be at Becky's at five-thirty.

Scott closed the cover on his phone and returned to the tour.

At three fifty-five Scott rang the doorbell at the Courtney residence, a magnificent antebellum mansion at the northernmost edge of the five-hundred-acre farm. Graceful white columns formed a two-story portico that always reminded Scott of *Gone With the Wind*. He could easily picture Scarlett O'Hara seated on a settee, batting her eyelashes behind her fan at a host of adoring beaux.

As he pressed the doorbell, he realized his cell phone was missing from his belt clip. He'd laid it down on the workbench this afternoon and forgot about it. Hopefully he'd have time to run back by the Pasture and pick it up before he went to Becky's.

The door opened, and Scott smiled a greeting at Marion, Lee's indispensable assistant.

"Right on time, as usual." Marion allowed him to press his lips to her cheek as he stepped inside. "He's out on the veranda. Do you remember the way?"

"I think so."

Scott had only been here a couple of times, but he'd been given the grand tour. Soft strains of classical music drifted down the wide, curving stairway, punctuated by the sound of his boots echoing on the tiled floor until he stepped into a carpeted den. There, eight-foot French doors that opened onto the veranda had been thrown wide to let a soft, rose-scented breeze flood the room. When he stepped outside, he found Lee seated in a white wicker chair, well shaded from the bright afternoon sunlight that bathed an enormous rose garden. Water trickled down multilayered porcelain bowls in a fountain in the center of the garden.

"Scott, there you are." The old gentleman laid his book on a glass-covered table beside him and stood to shake Scott's hand. "Have a seat."

As Scott sat in the chair he indicated, Marion stepped through the French doors bearing a tray.

"Ah, Marion, you always know what I want before I ask." Lee beamed up at her, his blue eyes twinkling beneath thick gray brows.

"Of course I do." She set the tray on the low table and winked at Scott. "That's why you keep me around."

She poured two tall glasses of lemonade from a frosty pitcher and set one before each of them. When she disappeared back into the house, Lee picked up his glass and held it to his lips.

He looked at Scott over the rim. "How are things going down at Out to Pasture?"

"Fine. I'm getting to know the horses and have spoken with most of the regular donors. You know, introduced myself, assured them that their help is still appreciated and necessary."

"Good, good."

Scott crossed his legs. "Several of them wanted to know when the board would meet to discuss the Pasture's future." Scott didn't mention that two donors had questioned him closely to determine if he was interested in taking the job as the Pasture's director on a permanent basis. He'd been flattered, but if he passed that along it would sound like bragging.

Lee sipped his lemonade, then held the glass in both hands and stared into it. "That's why I wanted to talk to you. I've had a few calls this morning from some of the board members."

So maybe he didn't have to blow his own horn after all. Maybe some of those donors had contacted the board on his behalf. He picked up his own glass and waited for Lee to continue.

"Frankly, Scott, they're concerned. They question my decision to put you in charge."

Scott sat immobile, searching the old man's face while his words sank in. Someone didn't think he could handle the job? Blood surged uncomfortably in his ears as the silence between them deepened.

He leaned forward to set his glass back on the table.

"I'm stunned. You might not remember this, but I have a lot of experience working with stallions."

Lee waved a hand. "Your experience isn't in question. Your maturity is."

"My maturity?" He shook his head. "I don't understand. Do they think I'm too young to handle the job?"

Lips pursed, Lee studied him. Scott resisted the urge to squirm beneath the older man's searching glance.

"I'll be honest with you. Neal excelled in many ways, but his personal habits were, shall we say, less than professional in some areas. Out to Pasture was his creation, his dream-child. But on more than one occasion his reputation had a negative impact on the organization."

Scott leaned back in his seat. "I can see how that would cause the board some concern. But what does it have to do with me? I don't have a bad reputation."

Lee moved his book to pick up the folded section of a newspaper beneath it. He held it toward Scott. "Have you seen this?"

Scott took it. A glance at the top showed him it was today's *Davidson County Post*. He started to tell Lee that he didn't take the small-town paper when his gaze caught on a headline.

## Man Strangled In His Own Home

He skimmed the account of Eddie Jones's death, exercising a huge amount of self-control to keep his face impassive when he found his own name mentioned. The reporter had spoken with someone at O'Grady's, probably the same person Detective Foster questioned.

…A witness, who wished to remain anonymous, told police that a few hours before his death Jones was seen at O'Grady's Tavern arguing with the manager of Out to Pasture, a farm for retired Thoroughbred stallions. Scott Lewis, who took over management of the retirement farm after the previous manger was murdered last week, was unavailable for comment.

"Nobody ever asked me for a comment." He looked into Lee's eyes, willing the man to believe him. "Honestly. I was there all day yesterday and today, and nobody from the paper has been by."

"I've already called Jeffries, the owner of the *Post*. He said no one answered the phone last night in the office."

"Has he ever heard of leaving a message?" Anger seeped into Scott's voice. Surely there were laws against this kind of treatment by the press. Even a small-town newspaper was subject to the law, wasn't it?

"Is it true?" Lee leaned forward to tap a finger on the article. "Do you associate with characters like this Jones?"

Scott flinched at the disapproval in the old gentleman's tone. He leaned forward, forearms resting on his thighs. "No, sir. I do not associate with Jones. The bare facts here are true, but I don't gamble at all, and I don't drink." He met Lee's gaze without flinching. "I went to the bar to ask him about the break-in because I thought he was responsible for it. He didn't like my questions, and got a little uptight. I wasn't even there ten minutes."

Lee's eyes narrowed as he subjected Scott to a soul-searching stare. Finally, he nodded once and sat back with a relieved smile. "I knew you'd have an explanation. I'm never wrong about a man's character."

Scott sagged with relief. He picked up his glass and gulped, more for an excuse to look away than because of thirst.

Lee took the paper from his unresisting hand and buried it beneath his book. "I'll give the board members a call, explain things. Don't worry about it."

"I appreciate that." Sensing that he was being dismissed, Scott stood.

Lee stood, as well, and extended his hand. "Thanks for coming by. The board is meeting on Friday, so I'll give you a call and let you know how it goes."

Scott found his way to the front door alone and exited the house. Frustration tensed his jaw as he stomped down the porch stairs. Thank goodness Lee believed him, and he'd explain Scott's involvement with Eddie Jones to the board. But what about the others who read that article?

He slid behind the wheel of his truck and slammed the door. Instead of turning the key in the ignition, he stared across the gentle swells of green farmland. He could just glimpse the roof of the Pasture beyond the Shady Acres horse barn.

He'd never had a boss express anything close to displeasure in him, and the experience rankled. He needed to keep his reputation spotless if he had any chance of landing a job at another Thoroughbred farm. Or, as he'd begun to consider, of keeping the job at Out to Pasture permanently. Who would hire him to manage a multimillion dollar enterprise if they thought he was reckless with his personal finances?

He shook himself as he turned the key. The engine roared to life. He was going to a prayer meeting tonight, and a good, long prayer was exactly what he needed.

But first, dinner with Becky and Jamie and Tyler. A

glance at his watch told him he had just enough time to get home, shower and get over to her house. She'd left work an hour early, probably to get dinner ready for him. He didn't care if she served tuna fish sandwiches and potato chips, he was just looking forward to an evening with her. Something about Becky relaxed him. She was so easy to talk to, so insightful and smart. He loved that ready smile that ignited her eyes.

He punched the gas pedal. If he hurried, he'd have time to stop and pick up some flowers, as he should have done last night.

# EIGHTEEN

$B$ecky checked the address on her note and compared it to the number etched in gold on the plaque in the front yard of what she could only describe as a modern mansion. Three elegant stories, tall graceful windows, glittering crystal in the wide double doors. She battled a fit of nerves as she turned onto the circular driveway. Maybe she should have called Isabelle first. The police might already have been here, and it would be so embarrassing to be thrown out on her ear. But if they hadn't questioned her yet, Becky wanted to warn her that they might be coming.

Feeling like a poor relation, she pulled her bedraggled car beneath the arched portico and cut the engine. She clutched the steering wheel, gathering her nerve, then got out of the car. She paused in the act of locking the doors. Nobody would bother breaking into her old Chevy in a ritzy neighborhood like this one.

The exquisite front door opened the moment her foot reached the topmost brick step. When it did, cigar-scented air rushed outward. A dark-haired man who seemed to be all legs looked down on her from a lofty height, his expression one of polite inquiry. When she noticed a slight flaring of his hawklike nostrils, Becky bit back a nervous giggle.

"I'm here to see Isabelle Keller. My name is Becky Dennison."

"I'm sorry," he said, in a voice that denied it, "but Miss Keller isn't home this afternoon."

She *knew* she should have called. She gave the man a bright smile. "Will you tell her I dropped by, and ask her to call me?"

"Lawrence, who're you talking to?" A man's deep voice sounded from somewhere inside the house.

Lawrence turned his head and spoke without moving. "Someone to see Miss Keller."

"Well, don't leave her standing outside. Bring her in."

Lawrence paused only a second, long enough for Becky to wish she'd taken the time to refresh her lipstick, then stepped backward and opened the door wider. Becky stepped into an entry hall that belonged in Buckingham Palace. Marble everywhere, on the floors, the staircase, the tops of antique tables scattered all around. When the door closed behind her, the late-afternoon sunlight pouring through the glass cast dancing rainbows across the floor.

Movement to her right drew her attention. A man stood from a wing chair and stooped over an ashtray to put out his cigar before coming toward her. This man wasn't much taller than Becky, with a thick neck and muscular arms that bulged like one of Jamie's toy action figures. She recognized him from the newspapers.

"Mr. Keller, my name is Becky Dennison. I'm a friend of Isabelle's."

His hand engulfed hers, and he studied her face with small, piercing eyes. "I don't think I've heard Izzy mention your name."

Becky fought the impulse to look away. "Actually, we just met last week when she stopped by the place I work."

"And where is that?"

"Out to Pasture. I work in the office."

Something flared in his eyes that made Becky want to take a step backward. But it was gone before she could identify it. "I see. Please come in and sit down." He gestured toward an empty wing chair on the other side of a marble-topped table from his. "Can I have Lawrence bring you a drink?"

As she sat, she noticed a half-full glass beside the ashtray. From the smell of it, it was something alcoholic. At four-fifteen in the afternoon?

She perched on the edge of the seat cushion, ankles crossed, and held her purse in her lap. "No, thank you. I can't stay long."

With a glance of dismissal at Lawrence, Mr. Keller reseated himself and turned to look at her full-on. "You're the one who found the money. In a bag of dog food, I heard."

Becky straightened. She didn't know the discovery was public information.

He must have seen her surprise, because he explained. "I have friends at State Police Headquarters in Frankfort."

She remembered what Scott said about charges against Mr. Keller always being dropped. "I see."

Ice clinked against the sides of his glass when he picked it up. "Did my Izzy talk to you, tell you she'd been seeing Haldeman?"

Becky watched his hand as he swirled the liquid. Those hands were huge, and strong. Strong enough to kill a man with a hoof pick? Or maybe strangle him in his sleep?

A tickle of fear made her palms begin to sweat. She wiped them on her slacks. "Yes, she did."

A blast of humorless laughter shook his shoulders. "He was toying with her. He did that, toyed with women just to get money out of them for those precious horses of his. I warned her, but she wouldn't listen." His jowls drooped as he stared at the carpet in front of his chair. When he spoke again, it was almost a whisper. "She wouldn't listen. And now what will happen to her?"

He knew. Becky was suddenly sure that Isabelle's father knew of her pregnancy.

"Mr. Keller," she said gently, "maybe he did toy with women in the past, but a man can change. Maybe Neal really loved Isabelle."

"Ha!" He jerked upright and some of the liquor splashed out of his glass onto his pants. He didn't appear to notice. "He didn't. Know how I know?"

The last came out slurred. The man was drunk.

*Lord, please get me out of here in one piece!*

Becky kept her voice calm, though fear was creeping up her spine to brush prickly fingers at the back of her neck. "How do you know?"

He went still, staring into her eyes for a long moment. "Because I paid him to leave her and the baby alone. Gave him two hundred fifty thousand dollars. And he took it." He held the glass to his lips, staring into it. "He took it."

"How long have you known about the baby?"

"Since Izzy found out. She took one of those test things, and left it in the trash can. Lawrence found it, brought it to me." He jerked his head upright and glared at her. "Don't tell her I know. I want her to come to me on her own."

Becky sat back in the chair. The money had come from Isabelle's father. A bribe. Not a horse race. Had Neal told his bookies he had the money to pay them off? Who knew about it besides Mr. Keller?

She leaned forward. "Did you break into Out to Pasture to get your money back?"

He put his head back and laughed. "You're smart, you are. You should work for the police. They wouldn't have been able to figure it out if I hadn't told 'em."

"You confessed?"

He shrugged. "It's okay. I turned over everything I took. Fifty bucks in cash, which made it look like a real robbery, and the files. I figured they'd be happy to get those records, once I saw what they were. They probably can't use it as evidence, but at least they have it." He shook his head. "Never thought to look in the dog food, though."

If he broke into the office, did he also break into the barn? She couldn't help staring at those strong hands.

He followed her glance and laughed. "No, I didn't kill him." He flexed his fingers into a fist. "I could have, I was that mad. But I figured paying him off was a better way. And I was right. Izzy will see that sooner or later. She didn't know about the others, she believed him when he told her he loved her. But I knew better. I had him watched. He was having an affair with a married woman at the same time he was seeing my Izzy."

"An affair?" Becky's clutch on her purse tightened. "Mr. Keller, do you know who he was seeing?"

"Of course." He set the drink down. "Leslie Stevens. His next-door neighbor's wife. The scumbag."

Becky's mouth fell open. No way! She had met Leslie several times, because she came to the Pasture often. She and her husband, Nick, were regular donors.

"Did you tell the police?"

He scowled. "Why should I? The woman has bad taste in men, but I see no sense in dragging her into a mess. Let the dead stay dead, and leave the living alone, that's my motto."

Becky watched him pick up his cigar, glance at her and put it down again. She stood.

"I really must be going, Mr. Keller. Please tell Isabelle I stopped by."

He didn't get out of the chair as Becky practically ran to the front door. She felt the weight of his stare on her back as she slipped outside, not breathing freely until she was in her car with the doors locked.

She glanced at her watch. She couldn't be late picking up the boys. The day care center charged a dollar a minute after closing time. And she had to get home to put dinner on before Scott arrived. Now's when she wished she had a cell phone, so she could call the police before the boys got in the car. She had to tell them she'd discovered the identity of the L in the note.

"What are we having?"

Jamie's tone, as usual, told Becky he expected the worst.

She'd managed to regain her composure before she arrived at the day care center by reminding herself that there was nothing time sensitive in the revelation of the mysterious L. She could pull Jeff Whitley aside at church tonight. That would be soon enough.

"Cheeseburgers, Tater Tots and a salad."

"Woo-hoo!" Tyler danced in his seat, arms pumping the air. Thank goodness for seat belts.

A glance in the rearview mirror showed her Jamie's scowl. "I don't like salad."

"I know you don't. But you can at least eat a tomato and a cucumber."

She grinned at his dramatic sigh of woe.

As she turned the corner onto her street, Becky looked automatically toward her house. Odd. There was an unfamiliar car in the driveway. And was that a man sitting on her front stoop?

Her pulse picked up speed as she slowed the car. Had Mr. Keller realized he'd talked too much? Did he send someone to her house to warn her to keep her mouth shut?

"Who's at our house?" asked Jamie.

"I don't know."

She'd drive right past, go around the block and leave. But where could she go? She faced forward while trying to get a look at the guy as she drove by. Maybe she'd go to Amber's house. Maybe—

Her foot slammed the brake pedal. The car came to a screeching halt just beyond her driveway. She knew that man.

She pulled forward to the curb in front of her next-door neighbor's house and parked.

When she turned off the engine, the rear door opened and Tyler tumbled out to the sidewalk, Jamie right behind. Becky jerked her door open and grabbed their shirts before they got three steps away from the car.

"You two stay here." She directed her sternest stare at both boys. "Do not move. Do you understand me?"

Her tone promised dire consequences, and they got the message. Wide-eyed, they nodded and backed up to lean against the car. She took a bracing breath and faced her house. This could *not* be happening. Not tonight. Not in front of the boys.

As she walked down the sidewalk, the man stood. "I thought that was you."

"Christopher, what are you doing here?"

"I came to see my wife and sons." He flashed the lopsided grin she remembered so well. Her stomach clenched in response.

"Ex-wife."

"Whatever."

He hopped down the concrete stairs and came toward her, arms extended. She took a step backward, warning him with a glare to keep his distance.

"Whoa, a little touchy, aren't you?"

"And why wouldn't I be?" She didn't even try to filter her tone. "Did you expect me to welcome you with open arms like nothing's happened? After *four years* without a word?"

His hands dropped to his sides. "Trust me, I wasn't any good for anybody these past few years. You wouldn't have wanted me around." His voice softened. "But a day hasn't gone by that I didn't think of you and the twins, Becky."

Was that actual contrition she heard in his voice? She eyed him suspiciously. Chris could charm a T-bone from a hungry bear. It was one of his talents.

"And now?"

He looked her straight in the eye. "I'm getting things back on track. I've got a steady job down in Florida doing landscaping for a big corporation." His shoulders jerked with a silent laugh. "They actually pay me to dig in the dirt. Turns out I'm good at something after all. Wouldn't my old man have been surprised if he'd lived?"

Becky fought against a wave of sympathy, which made her angry. She didn't want to feel sorry for the man who deserted her with two little babies. "You were good at lots of things," she said, grudgingly. "Just not good at sticking with them."

"Yeah, well, that's all changing." He craned his neck toward her car. "Are those the boys? I'll bet I won't even recognize them."

Oh, he'd recognize them all right. He saw them every day in the mirror. Becky realized anew how much her sons looked like their father.

"I wish you had called first, Christopher. They were babies when you left. They don't remember you. I need to prepare them."

"Prepare them for what? I'm their father." His smile tightened. "I figure since I'm paying child support, I might as well exercise my visitation rights."

She spoke through clenched teeth. "You don't pay for the privilege of seeing your children. You pay for the responsibility of raising them. And you haven't done your fair share of that."

"I know, I know." He held his hands out, fingers splayed, and took another step toward her. "Are we going to argue about this right now? I've come a long way, and I'd like to see my sons." His arms dropped to his sides and he tried another smile on her. "I've looked forward to seeing you, too, Becky. I've really missed you."

For one instant, time stopped. A bird in a distant tree fell silent. The light breeze that tickled her hair stilled. Even her heart seemed to pause in her chest.

How many times had she dreamed of hearing those words from Christopher? She fell in love with him on the first day of their freshman year in high school, and had never loved another. After he left she'd lost count of the number of nights her aching heart kept her awake in bed, knowing he would never share it again. Why should he, when so many other women welcomed him to theirs?

The wind stirred the grass at her feet. The bird resumed its song. Her heart thudded to life. The Lord had soothed her hurts, healed the wounds Christopher had inflicted. But the scars remained, and they were a little more tender than she'd realized.

"I'm a Christian now, Chris. I live a different life than the one we shared."

A scowl drew his eyebrows together. "Your father got to you, did he?"

She smiled. He always disliked Daddy. And the feeling was definitely mutual. "Yes, my Father got to me. But not the one you think."

"Mommy?" They both turned to look at her car. Tyler had taken a few steps toward them. "Can we go in the house now? Jamie's gotta go to the bathroom."

"Would you look at him!" Christopher's face broke into a wide grin of genuine delight.

Before she could react, he ran down the sidewalk and stopped in front of them, his arms thrown wide. "Hey, you guys. It's me, your long lost daddy."

The look Tyler threw her way was pure confusion. If only she'd had time to talk to them first, tell them what to expect. She infused her smile with as much confidence as she could, and nodded at him.

Christopher picked Tyler up and whirled him around. "You play ball, don't you?"

The boy looked uncertainly toward her. "We just started T-ball."

"I thought so. Look at that." He squeezed the muscle on Tyler's arm. "That's the arm of a ballplayer if I ever saw one."

Becky reached the car as Christopher bent down to eye-level in front of Jamie. "How 'bout you, big guy? Do you play ball, too?"

Jamie nodded slowly, his dark eyes suspicious.

Christopher straightened. "Good, because I brought you guys a present."

Tyler's expression lightened. "What kind of present?"

"Everything you need to set up your own practice field in the backyard. A real batting tee, and helmets, and a practice screen, a glove for each of you, and a couple of real Louisville Slugger bats."

Becky bit back a sarcastic comment about the cost of all that equipment. Apparently having his paycheck garnisheed hadn't reduced him to poverty level.

Tyler was duly impressed. "Wow!" He did a victory dance on the sidewalk.

Jamie wasn't as easy to win over. "I already have a glove."

"Not like this one, buddy." Christopher's face lit with enthusiasm. "This is made out of top-grade premium steer hide, with extra padding in the palm to protect your hand from stinging line drives."

"Where is it?" Tyler raced toward their driveway. "Is that your car?"

Christopher straightened and called after Tyler. "Yep. Drove it all the way from Florida. That's where I live, right down the street from Disney World."

Jamie's gaze flicked from Becky to his father. "You live by Disney World?"

Christopher was pushing, true, but at least he seemed to be pushing the right buttons.

He grinned at Jamie. "That's right. But I haven't ever been. I've been waiting until you guys could go with me."

She cast a look of warning his way. He was good at making promises he couldn't keep. She wouldn't stand by and watch him disappoint her sons.

"Come on. Let's go put up the practice screen." He held out a hand toward Jamie.

The boy hesitated, looking toward his mother as though for permission. What could she do? He had been a louse of a husband, and a completely absent parent. But he was their father.

She unclenched her jaw enough to give Jamie a reassuring smile. "Let's do that."

Christopher grinned with triumph when Jamie clasped his hand. Together they jogged down the sidewalk, Becky following slowly behind.

Twenty minutes later, the doorbell rang.

"I'll get it," shouted both boys.

"No, let me."

Becky rushed to grab a paper towel to wipe the raw hamburger off her hands. She'd tried to call Scott, to explain why she had to cancel their plans this evening. But she wasn't able to get him on his cell.

She stepped into the living room, still wiping her hands, to find that Jamie had beaten her to the door. Scott stood on the front stoop, holding a bouquet of spring flowers. His eyes locked on to hers, and the smile that spread across his face warmed a cold spot deep inside that had appeared the moment she saw Chris on her doorstep.

Then Scott looked down. The living room was covered with packages and baseball paraphernalia. Christopher and Tyler knelt before a metal frame, the netting on the floor ready to be stretched on.

At the sight of Christopher, Scott's expression froze.

Becky stood speechless as Christopher got to his feet, stepped around the packages and approached the door.

"Hi, I'm Christopher Dennison." He extended his hand toward Scott. "Becky's husband."

Scott's gaze sought hers. The hand holding the flowers dropped to his side. She had never seen a face so full of pain.

She took a step forward, reaching toward him. "Scott, let me—"

He didn't wait to hear her explanation. Helplessly, she watched him turn on his heel and walk away.

Becky swallowed against a lump of tears that had lodged in her throat as she placed the receiver back in its cradle. Scott wasn't answering his phone. Not that she blamed him for dodging her calls, but if only he would let her explain.

She shook her head. Explain what? What could she say that would erase the pain, the look of betrayal he had given her? She covered her face with her hands and pressed against her eyeballs. She would never be able to forget the look on his face, the flowers thrown into the front yard, the screech of his tires as he zoomed out of her driveway.

"Hey, you okay in here?"

She dropped her hands at the sound of Chris's voice, and turned away so he wouldn't see the tears in her eyes. "I'm fine. Are the boys in bed?"

"Yeah. Thanks for letting me tuck them in." He scooted a chair out from the table. "I even listened to them say their prayers."

Becky picked up the damp dishcloth hanging over the faucet and swiped it over the already spotless countertop. "That's good."

"So, did you get your boyfriend on the phone?"

The sarcasm in his voice made her whirl toward him. "He's not my boyfriend," she snapped. She didn't bother to hide her anger as she continued. "And you are not my husband, Chris. Why did you say that?"

"Hey, calm down." He threw up a hand as though to ward her off. "I was just trying to—"

"To what? Scare him off?" Her pulse pounded with barely suppressed rage as she glared at him. "You have no right to even talk to my friends. You show up here after all these years and expect to step right in where you left off. Well, trust me, that is not going to happen."

The last came out in a hiss as Becky tried to keep her voice down so the boys wouldn't hear her from their bedroom.

Chris rose from the table and crossed the floor in two steps. She backed up until she was pressed against the sink, a thrill of fear coursing through her. Would he hurt her? Chris had never gotten physical with her during even the stormiest part of their marriage. He wouldn't start now, would he?

No, that look on his face wasn't anger. It was something else, something equally alarming.

He spoke softly. "Becky, I'm sorry. I don't know what came over me when that guy walked through the door. I think I was jealous."

He inched forward, and she leaned backward as far as she could. Even so, she felt his breath on her cheek when he whispered, "I want you back, Becky. I love you."

# NINETEEN

When Becky's car pulled into the driveway Thursday morning, Scott's jaw clenched. He kept his gaze fixed on the halter he was cleaning while Sam leaped off his bed and ran to greet her. If she had any sense of decency at all, she'd head for the office without trying to talk to him.

"Scott."

So much for decency.

He kept cleaning.

"Please let me explain."

He forced his tone to remain cool, to deny the heat that tried to creep into his throat. "No explanation needed. Your husband came back. End of story."

"He's my ex-husband."

Apparently the guy didn't appreciate the distinction. But Scott didn't want to argue with her. He kept his teeth clamped shut.

She took a step into the barn. Out of the corner of his eye, he saw her hands twist around each other. "I haven't seen him in over four years. I had no idea he even knew where we lived anymore."

He risked a glance at her face. Her eyes pleaded with him to understand. Just like Megan's had done. Oh, man, he'd been here before, and it wasn't any easier the second time around.

"And he showed up out of the blue begging you to take him back."

She blanched. "Something like that."

Scott set the halter down on the workbench and rubbed his eyes. They itched from a long, sleepless night where he replayed the scene in Becky's living room over and over in his mind. It was like the rerun of a pathetically sad movie. He was the lovelorn sucker fated to have his heart broken by the heroine. He couldn't figure out why God kept letting him fall for women destined to return to their husbands.

Part of him wanted to believe in Becky, in her inherent goodness and kindness. The guy he'd seen last night didn't look like someone she'd be attracted to. His sarcastic grin looked as though it could hide a cruel streak. But some women seemed to fall for men who hurt them. He just didn't think she'd turn out to be one of them.

He had to know one thing, though.

"Do you love him?"

A cricket chirped from the corner of the barn, its rhythmic song amplified by the silence between them. Becky couldn't look at Scott's face. She'd agonized over that question all night after Chris left to go back to his hotel.

"Yesterday I would have said no, without hesitation."

Scott dipped his head, forcing her to look up at him. "But today?"

"I don't think I know what love is anymore." Unshed tears clogged her throat. "My marriage was a mistake from the beginning. He didn't want a family, didn't want kids. All he wanted to do was party and have fun. He didn't change. I did. When I got pregnant, I wanted to settle down." Her fingers dug into the flesh on her arms. "But he says he's grown-up, and he wants his family back."

"And you think he deserves a second chance?"

His gaze seemed to penetrate to her soul. She didn't look away, but let him see all the pain and uncertainty that had kept her tossing and turning throughout the night. "Everyone gets a second chance, whether they deserve it or not. That's what Jesus is all about."

Now it was his turn to look away. He went back to the bench, picked up the strip of leather he'd been toying with when she arrived. "Well, I hope it works out for you. I'm sure the boys will enjoy having their parents back together again."

Pain squeezed her chest as she watched his profile. Why did Christopher have to pick now to resurface? *Lord, it's just not fair!*

Or maybe it was God's timing. Maybe He sent Chris back to stop her from developing a relationship with Scott.

Sam nosed at her hand, a not-so-subtle reminder that he hadn't eaten breakfast. She started to turn toward the house, then realized she needed to tell Scott about yesterday.

"I almost forgot. I found out something important."

He turned a look of polite inquiry her way, and she bit back another wave of sorrow. She would probably never see his warm smile again.

She filled him in on Mr. Keller.

His eyebrows arched when she revealed the identity of the mysterious L. "So did you call the police?"

"No. I was going to, but then I realized they'd show up at her house. What if her husband doesn't know about the affair?" She nudged a clump of dirt with the toe of her shoe. "I'd just hate to be the cause of another wrecked marriage."

"So what are you going to do?"

Becky had thought about that in the middle of the night, too. "I'm going to go see Leslie this morning. I'll tell her what I heard, and urge her to go to the police on her own."

Scott studied her a moment, then gave a nod. "I'll go with you."

"Oh, you don't have to do that." The conversation would be awkward enough without a man there.

But he refused to budge. "There's a murderer running around loose, and for all we know, he's aware of their affair. It might be dangerous. I can't let you go alone."

As she walked toward the house, Sam racing in front of her, Becky admitted that she felt relieved not to have to face Leslie Stevens alone.

The Stevens farm was only half the size of Shady Acres, but what Nick Stevens lacked in space, he made up for in flamboyance. Becky drove by every morning on her way to work and loved gazing at the elegant horse barns, with their spired roofs and candy-cane paint job. A new one had been erected right after she came to work at the Pasture, and she'd been amazed at how quickly it came together. A beautiful clear pond fronted the property, hidden jets spraying water high into the sky to be caught by the wind and sprinkled on the crystal surface.

Becky rang the doorbell twice at the Stevens home, but no one answered.

Scott shielded his eyes from the bright April sunshine and looked over the grounds. "Let's see if she's down at the barn. There are several cars over that way."

"I hope Nick isn't there." Becky hopped up into the pickup. "What will we say if he is?"

Scott lifted a shoulder as he started the engine. "He probably won't be. I think he spends a lot of time at his office in Lexington. But if he is, I'll keep him busy while you get Leslie off in a corner somewhere."

Beyond a large pasture where a half-dozen yearlings grazed, they drove by a couple of small paddocks, each with its own resident horse. One ran along the fence on Becky's side, keeping pace with the truck, and she admired the way the muscles rippled along its hindquarters.

"Hey, that's a stallion." She turned to look at Scott. "I didn't realize the Stevenses kept stallions."

"Oh, yeah. They board three studs and manage a syndicate. Lee Courtney owns shares in a couple of them."

Neal had spoken of syndicates that owned and bred stallions, but Becky had only a vague knowledge of the process. All she knew was that Neal had identified a couple of horses owned by syndicates that were close to retiring, and he hoped the owners would send them to the Pasture when they stopped producing.

They turned the corner at the end of the paddock, and Scott inched past three horse trailers parked along the fencerow.

"Looks like they're busy today," he commented. "You might have a hard time getting Leslie's attention. She's pretty involved at the breeding shed."

Breeding? A flush crept up Becky's neck. She hadn't anticipated walking in on horses breeding with Scott there. In the months since coming to work at the Pasture she'd learned enough about the Thoroughbred industry to know those involved in the breeding process viewed it with a clinical, businesslike detachment. But she hadn't managed to develop that attitude yet.

She turned away when her cheeks started to warm. "Maybe we should come back later."

Thank goodness Scott didn't seem to notice her discomfort. "We're here. Might as well see if she's in." He got out of the truck.

Fighting to control the flush that she was sure had turned her face scarlet, Becky hopped to the ground and followed him into the small barn that was, apparently, a breeding shed.

It was bigger inside than she had expected, probably twice as big as the barn over at the Pasture, but instead of sweet hay, the place smelled of horse sweat. There were people everywhere. Three men surrounded a chestnut-colored mare, one with a firm grip on her halter while the other two rubbed her neck and spoke in low, soothing voices. Someone stooped behind her doing who-knew-what, while someone else stood to one side holding a small camcorder. Beyond the open back door came the sound of impatient neighing.

To the right of the door, two men bent over a desk, flipping through papers. One straightened at their approach. "May I help you with something?"

Scott thrust a hand toward him. "Scott Lewis. I'm the manager of Out to Pasture. This is Becky Dennison, who works with me."

"Jason Rawlins." He shook Scott's hand and nodded a smile in Becky's direction. "Nice to meet you."

"I heard Stevens had a new manager," Scott said. "Sorry I haven't made it over to say hello."

He dismissed Scott's apology with a shrug. "I haven't managed to get out much myself. I figured things would be busy here, but nothing like it has been."

Jason looked toward the mare, who whinnied and

pranced in a circle. The man holding her halter skipped along with her, speaking in a low voice.

Why did Scott look so suspicious all of a sudden? He gestured in the horse's direction, but he kept a close watch on Jason. "She's a beauty. And unique. You don't see nite-eyes like that very often."

Becky looked at the horse. She was pretty, as far as Becky's uneducated opinion went. But nite-eyes? How could he tell, when it was daytime?

Jason looked as confused as Becky felt. But he didn't admit it, either. His gaze flicked to the mare, then back at Scott. "Yeah. Real unique."

Scott's lips pursed, and he studied Jason through narrowed eyes. "So, have you been in the business long?"

"Long enough." Jason cast a quick glance behind him. "Are you here as witnesses?"

Becky spoke quickly, in case Scott should decide they could stay and be witnesses as the mare was bred. "We're looking for Leslie."

"Oh." Jason glanced around the barn. "She was here a minute ago. She must have stepped out back to check on the stallion."

He seemed embarrassed, eager to get rid of them. His head jerked toward the desk, where the man he'd been talking to when they came in waited patiently for him to return. "You can go on out there and see if she's around."

Becky grabbed Scott's arm and pulled him toward the rear exit. "Thanks. We'll do that."

They stepped into the sunshine, and walked a few steps away from the barn.

Scott glanced behind him and spoke in a low voice. "Something's not right about that guy."

"He seemed okay to me."

"It's breeding season. Why would he be surprised at being busy? And I don't think he knows what nite-eyes are."

"So?" Becky tilted her head and admitted, "Neither do I."

"You're not managing a breeding shed." He shook his head. "Nite-eyes are growths on the inside of the knees. No two horses have identical nite-eyes. That guy obviously didn't know that."

"Shh." Becky dipped her head in the direction of a woman coming toward them.

Leslie Stevens walked with a confident stride that swung her dark ponytail, pulled through the back loop of a white cap. Becky had liked Leslie since the time she welcomed Becky to her new job as Neal's secretary with the gift of a vanilla-scented candle. She said it would, "give the place a woman's touch." Becky had been pleased by the gesture, especially coming from a wealthy horse breeder and one of the Pasture's major donors. Looking back on that incident now, she wondered if the gift had been a bribe to keep Becky's mouth shut in case someone questioned Leslie's close friendship with Neal.

Recognition showed on Leslie's face as she approached, and Becky thought her smile faded a fraction when they locked eyes, although that could have been her imagination.

Leslie smiled at Scott when she came close enough to shake his hand. "I've been meaning to stop by and congratulate you on your new position. Well deserved, I'm sure." She sobered. "Even though it came about under sad circumstances."

"Temporary position," Scott corrected.

"Not for long, I'll bet. The board would be insane to let you get away. You're exactly what the Pasture needs."

Becky agreed, but they had more pressing matters to discuss this morning. "Leslie, we need to talk to you about something important."

Fear darkened the eyes that turned Becky's way. She knew what was coming, Becky was sure of it.

"I expected the police. Not you." Her voice was heavy with dread. "I guess it was only a matter of time before the gossip chain started buzzing."

"We didn't hear about your relationship with Neal through gossip." Becky watched her face, saw confirmation there instead of denial. "Hugh Keller told me."

"Isabelle's father." Leslie shook her head sadly. "That poor girl. I told Neal not to hurt her. She was too vulnerable to get involved with someone like him."

Scott glanced at Becky before speaking. "The police found a handwritten note in Neal's truck, arranging a meeting for the night he was killed."

Leslie's shoulders sagged, and tears sprang to her eyes. "I figured they would. Given the circumstances, slipping Neal a note wasn't my smartest move."

Two men came out of the shed and headed toward the paddock where a stallion pranced and tossed his head. She turned slightly so they wouldn't see her tears. An unexpected wave of compassion washed over Becky at the grief apparent in the woman's face, and she stepped sideways to block her from view.

"You really cared for Neal, didn't you?"

Leslie didn't answer immediately. Her lips trembled as she lifted her chin to look out over the pasture behind Becky. Finally, she nodded. "He was easy to fall for. So outgoing, so passionate about his work. But we were wrong to have an affair." Her struggle to hold back her tears contorted her face. "I cared for Neal, but I do love my husband."

"You have a strange way of showing it." Disgust twisted Scott's features.

Leslie blanched, then nodded. "I made a terrible mistake. Nicky deserves better. The night Neal was killed, I was going to break it off. I did break it off. I went to his house around eleven-thirty, after Nicky was in bed." Her lips twisted in a humorless smile. "That was our regular routine."

"Was he alive then?" Becky asked, her voice low.

She nodded. "I told him I couldn't see him anymore. He said he understood. He knew it was the right thing to do. But while we were talking, one of the horses got really agitated. Neal turned off the lights so we could see outside, and we saw a figure run toward the barn."

"Could he tell who it was?" Scott asked.

She shook her head. "It was too dark. I was afraid Nicky had followed me, that he had caught us just when I was trying to make things right. But instead of coming to the house, whoever it was went into the barn. We saw a dim light, like a flashlight. Neal thought it must have been someone breaking in."

Becky was beginning to get the picture. "So Neal went out to surprise them, leaving Sam in the house to protect you."

Fresh tears welled in her eyes as she nodded. "I waited a long time, but he never came back. Finally, I couldn't stand the suspense anymore. I tiptoed out to the barn, and that's when I saw his body." She bent forward and buried her face in her hands. "He was dead. There was so much blood."

Scott still eyed her with suspicion. "Why didn't you call the police?"

Becky knew the answer before she gave it.

"I know I should have, but I panicked! Nicky would have to know, and what's the point in that? The affair was over." She looked from Becky to Scott, begging them understand. "You're not going to tell him, are you? He'll be devastated."

Becky placed a hand on her arm. "Of course we're not."

"But you need to go to the police." Scott's voice was hard.

Leslie's gaze flew to his face. "I can't do that!"

"You really have to, Leslie." Becky tried to infuse as much persuasion into her voice as possible. "They found the note and your footprints in the barn. It's only a matter of time before they find out about your relationship with Neal, just as I did. Then they'll come to question you, maybe in front of your husband."

Leslie closed her eyes, her face a mask of pain. She drew a shuddering breath, and gave a single nod. "You're right. I'll call them this morning."

# TWENTY

"We should tell the police ourselves."

Becky had never seen Scott so stubborn.

They sat at their desks in the office at the Pasture, Scott scowling across the room at her, his legs spread out before him. Becky struggled to control her rising temper. The man didn't have a compassionate bone in his body.

"She said she'd call them. I believe her."

His eyes rose to the ceiling. "You're too trusting."

"And you're too suspicious."

"She's an adulterer and a liar. Her husband deserves to know. I don't understand why you want to protect her."

Becky winced. Maybe she was being a little too soft on Leslie. But Leslie had realized her mistake. She'd taken steps to end her affair. What was wrong with wanting to protect her marriage from a devastating blow? Becky understood. She'd suffered the devastation of a failed marriage herself. She certainly didn't want to do anything to sabotage someone else's.

"I'll talk to Jeff at church on Sunday," she promised. "If she hasn't called them by then, I'll tell him."

Arms folded across his chest, Scott inhaled a long, slow breath. "I'll tell you who I'm suspicious of. Jason Rawlins."

Honestly, he seemed to have taken a real dislike to the poor guy. "Just because he doesn't have a lot of experience is no reason to suspect him of murder."

"How could someone with almost no experience land a job managing a breeding shed with someone as important as Nick Stevens?" He shook his head. "It just doesn't make sense. I wonder if Nick even knows what an idiot the guy is. He seems to leave the day-to-day running of the farm to Leslie."

"Well, Leslie is no dummy. If Jason didn't know what he was doing, she would see it."

Scott gave her a sad smile. "Some women are way too soft when it comes to men with a string of excuses."

Becky looked down so he couldn't see her cringe. So that's what the foul mood was all about. "Scott, I've said I'm sorry. What more do you want from me? Do you want me to find another job?"

"Of course not." He stood and strode across the room to the doorway, avoiding her gaze. "I'm probably not going to be around here much longer anyway."

What did he mean by that? Would he actually quit because of her? She couldn't let that happen.

"Scott, wait."

He stopped, but didn't turn to face her.

"You need to know something. Christopher lives in Florida." She bit her lip. She hated what she was about to say. "If we get back together, the boys and I will have to move there. So please don't leave the Pasture because of me."

She couldn't see his face, but the muscles in his shoulders tensed. A red flush stained the skin on the back of his neck.

"Don't worry. It won't be because of you."

What in the world did he mean by that? She didn't get

the chance to ask him to explain, because he hurried out of the room. At the sound of the back door slamming, Becky lowered her face into her hands and fought a wave of tears.

"He says he's changed, Daddy." Becky sliced into a piece of mail, the phone propped on her shoulder. "I think maybe he's grown up."

She'd sent him an e-mail first thing this morning, giving him the news of Christopher's return. She wasn't surprised when her phone rang at exactly eight-thirty California time.

"I don't believe it."

A check fluttered out of the envelope when she extracted a letter. She added it to a short pile of others. "You wouldn't. You never liked Chris."

"For very good reasons. He's a troublemaker who got my little girl suspended from school."

In the center of the room, Sam slept sprawled on the floor in a shaft of sunlight. He whimpered, his legs jerking in response to some dreamworld canine crisis.

She chuckled into the phone. "That was ten years ago, and I was just as guilty of skipping school as he was." But Daddy would prefer to blame someone else than acknowledge that his only daughter used to have a wild streak.

"A leopard doesn't change his spots, sweetheart. Especially a no-good, two-timing leopard."

"I changed my spots," she reminded him. "They've been washed clean."

"Has he become a Christian?"

She thought of the way Chris's face hardened last night when she told him she'd accepted the Lord. "No."

"Well, then, he's still a loser. Tell him to hit the road."

She tsked in his ear. "That isn't a very Christian attitude."

"I'll pray for him." From his tone, Becky didn't want to know what Daddy would ask the Lord to do with Christopher. "But that doesn't mean I want him hanging around my little girl. Or my grandsons."

She sobered. Laying down the letter opener, she rested a hand on the desk as she spoke into the phone. "He's their father. All the books stress how important it is for kids to have a relationship with their fathers. Even men who are not especially good parents. Jamie and Tyler will have to learn to deal with him sooner or later." Her voice became soft, remembering how the boys clung to Chris when he left last night. "But I think he could be a good father, given the opportunity. You should have seen them, Daddy. He got down on the floor and played with them, and they loved it." Amber's words came back to her. "They need a man around. They're starved for male attention."

"Then move them out here," he bellowed.

Wincing, she jerked the phone away from her ear. "Even if they were all the way on the other side of the country, Christopher would still be their father." She closed her eyes. "And my ex-husband."

Cell phone static crackled during a long pause.

"You're not thinking of going back to that jerk, are you?" His voice became stern. "Rebecca Ann, don't you even consider it. I'll come out there and turn you over my knee."

She laughed. "I'd like to see you try. Listen, Daddy, I've got to go. We've got a tour scheduled at noon, and a car just pulled into the driveway."

"I'll call you tonight. We're going to finish this conversation."

"After nine, okay? Love you, Daddy."

"Love you, sweetheart."

Becky replaced the receiver. For a moment she didn't move, just stared at the telephone. If she reconciled with Chris, Daddy would be furious.

But Tyler and Jamie deserved to have a relationship with both of their parents. And they were her first priority. As their mother, she had to put their welfare above her own. Didn't she owe them the opportunity to grow up with a father who loved them? Who loved her, even if she wasn't sure she returned his affection any longer?

After Chris left last night she had taken her Bible to bed and poured through the pages. The concordance in the back pointed her to the part that said an unbelieving husband could be won over by his wife, and her heart sank when she read it.

But she wasn't his wife anymore! If they hadn't divorced, her choice would be clear. She would stay with Chris and pray that God would reach him through her. But they *had* divorced. Did God want her to reconcile with a spouse who wasn't a Christian?

Her nails bit into the soft part of her hand as she banged a fist on the desk. It wasn't fair! She had needs, too. Didn't she deserve to be with someone she could love whole-heartedly? Would her mistakes of the past continue to reach into her future, to make her miserable?

Angry tears prickled in her eyes. In the old days, God sent an angel or a prophet so there was no question about what He wanted them to do. If only He would send a messenger to her now, to point her in the right direction.

She snatched a tissue from the box on her desk and scrubbed at her eyes.

It was the guessing that would drive her crazy.

\* \* \*

"I don't like those green things," Jamie informed the server at the pizza restaurant.

He sat in the booth on Christopher's right, Tyler on the left. Alone on the opposite bench, Becky glanced up at the woman, who stood with her pen poised over an order pad, then back down at Chris. "We usually get half with double cheese and half with pepperoni and sausage."

With a grin, he slapped the menu closed. "Those are my two favorites. Bring us an extra large. And a pitcher of beer."

Becky couldn't believe her ears. What was he doing? She leveled a hard stare across the table, nodding toward Jamie.

"What?" Chris affected an injured expression. "Okay, fine. You can drive. Here."

He tossed his car keys across the table. They slid off the edge and dropped into her lap.

"Chris, I don't think it's a good—"

He stopped her with a look. "Not a big deal, unless you turn it into one."

She glanced at Tyler, who was watching her with a puzzled expression. All the parenting books said it was vital that parents not argue in front of the children, that it damaged their sense of security. So far she'd never had to heed that advice— there'd been no one to argue with. But she planned to discuss this with Christopher later, when the boys were in bed.

She smiled up at the woman. "I'll have a Diet Coke, and they'll each have a Sprite."

Their order duly recorded, the server left. Chris leaned back, put a hand on each twin's head and rumpled their hair. "So, what do you say we go to the ball field tomorrow and practice running the bases?"

"Yeah!" Tyler turned an eager face toward her. "Can we, Mommy?"

"I have to work until five, but after that we could."

Chris shook his head. "It'll have to be during the day. I've got plans tomorrow night." He winked at her. "Can't come to town and not get together with my old buds, can I? But I could pick up the boys after school and drop them off when you get home. You know, my first official visitation, like the court says I get."

Becky shifted on the padded bench, not meeting Chris's eyes. He was right. The court said he could have the boys one night a week and every other weekend. But he'd never exercised that right, not wanting the responsibility of caring for two babies. Still, if she agreed, she'd have to sign a form giving him permission to pick up the boys from school. She wasn't ready to do that just yet.

The server arrived with their drinks and placed them on the table. Chris immediately poured beer into a frosty glass mug and chugged half of it. The pungent smell brought back a dozen memories of the old days. None of them good.

Becky toyed with the car keys and tried not to look disapproving. What did he have going on tomorrow night? Was he meeting up with one of his old girlfriends? Suspicion burned in her mind, and she hated it. When she was pregnant, she'd caught him with other women so often she'd been reduced to a raving maniac whenever he said he was going anywhere without her. That life had been long ago, but the old feelings resurfaced with surprising speed.

Would it be different this time around? It would have to be. Chris knew his sons now. Surely he'd want to be a positive influence in their lives. He probably was just going to see some of his old friends, as he said. She shouldn't jump to conclusions.

"Hey, look, there's one of those claw games." Chris leaned against the back of the booth to straighten his legs so he could dig in his pocket. He dropped a handful of change on the table. "I've got some quarters. Let's go play. I'll show you how to win, guaranteed every time."

Tyler took off across the restaurant at a gallop, Chris right behind him, the beer mug in his hand. Jamie slid out of the booth more slowly. Instead of following his brother and father, he stood at the edge of the table, his face solemn, staring at the pitcher.

He spoke in a quiet voice. "Mommy, is that drugs?"

Startled, Becky's gaze flew to his face. Where had her five-year-old heard about drugs? Were they already teaching drug prevention in kindergarten?

And how should she answer? He'd just seen his father take a big drink. She jingled the keys in her lap, uncomfortable, and forced a smile to her face. "No, sweetie, that's not drugs. It's beer. Grown-ups sometimes drink beer."

"Do you?"

She shook her head. "No, I don't."

Thank goodness Jamie didn't press the matter. He nodded slowly, then turned toward the claw machine.

His face lit up. "Hey, there's Mr. Lewis!"

Becky's heart thudded in her chest as Jamie took off at a run. Scott, here?

"Mr. Lewis!"

A dark-haired missile darted toward him and tackled his thighs. Startled, Scott looked down at Jamie Dennison, then up at the man standing next to a toy machine. Becky's ex-husband. Just his luck to run into Dennison at the town's only pizza restaurant. Next time, he'd let them deliver.

"Hey, Jamie, what are you doing here?"

The little boy tilted his head back to look up at Scott. "We're getting pizza. Cheese for me, and pepperoni for Tyler."

Focused on the game, Tyler said, "Hi, Mr. Lewis," but didn't take his hands off the controls.

"Well, if it isn't my wife's boss." Becky's ex straightened and put an arm on the top of the machine. He leaned against it, a smirk on his face. Instead of washing his hair, he'd pulled it back in a ponytail tonight, not a nice look, in Scott's opinion. His other hand held a mug of beer. Startled, Scott eyed him carefully. Surely the idiot wasn't planning to drive his sons home after drinking beer. Maybe he should make a phone call to Trooper Whitley to tip him off.

A movement in the center of the restaurant drew his attention. Becky rose from a booth and turned slowly. Tension tightened her features, but as she locked eyes with him, he thought he saw a flicker of relief. His throat constricted as she gave him a hesitant smile.

*Lord, she's so pretty, so sweet. What's she doing with a jerk like this?*

"Is Sam here?"

Scott tore his gaze away from Becky and looked down at her son. Jamie searched behind him, as though expecting to find the dog following along.

"He's waiting in the truck."

"Can I go see him?"

Dennison put a hand on the boy's shoulder, his gaze fixed on Scott. "Not right now, *son*."

Scott ignored him and smiled into Jamie's disappointed face. "Another time."

He went to the counter and gave the cashier his name. Thank goodness, his pizza was ready and waiting. He tossed a twenty toward the woman. Just get him out of there fast.

Becky stepped up beside him. He didn't look at her, but out of the corner of his eye he saw her hands clutching at each other.

"Scott, I'm so sorry."

The woman counting out his change was taking way too long. He watched as she peeled open a new roll of pennies with agonizing precision.

"Sorry for what? For wanting a pizza?"

"No, for…" She glanced over her shoulder.

Scott followed her gaze in time to see Dennison drain his beer mug. He turned a hard look on Becky. "I hope you're not drinking, too."

She stiffened. "Of course I'm not."

Finally, the cashier held his change toward him. He shoved it into his pocket without looking at it, picked up the pizza box and turned toward the door.

Dennison stepped into his path. "What's your hurry, Lewis? Why don't you join us for a beer?"

Excitement lit Jamie's and Tyler's faces. Beside him, Becky uttered a sound of protest.

Scott clamped his jaw shut against a sharp retort, but managed a stiff, "Thanks anyway."

Dennison lifted his empty mug in farewell. "Another time, then."

*Yeah. Next time a mule wins the Derby.*

Vowing to give up pizza for as long as he lived in this small town, Scott made his escape.

# TWENTY-ONE

The minute Becky's car came to a stop, the back doors flew open and the boys tumbled out. She took her time gathering her purse and her nerve, glancing through the windshield to watch them run toward Scott in the barn.

She stood in time to hear Tyler explain, "Dad's going to pick us up in a few minutes, so we can't help you feed the horses today. But we can throw the ball to Sam till he gets here."

"Here it is!" Jamie raced over to the dog's blanket, stooped and held the ball aloft.

Sam danced in a circle, which set both boys laughing. They ran off toward the grass to begin their game.

Becky stepped up to the barn's entrance but didn't go inside. "I stopped to get them on the way back from the vet's office." She held the bag of ointment toward him, proof that she'd been on an official errand. "I just didn't think it was a good idea to let their father pick them up at school."

Scott came toward her slowly, his eyes searching her face with an intensity that made her stomach flip-flop. "Why isn't that a good idea?"

She gulped, and her gaze dropped to her shoes. "I'm not sure why."

"Well, I think—"

Whatever he thought remained unsaid. Tyler's voice interrupted. "Jamie, I'm telling! You're not supposed to go in there!"

Becky turned to see what misdeed Jamie was performing. Her heart skipped a beat.

There was her older son, crawling between the two bottom fence planks into Alidor's paddock.

In the far corner, the stallion raised his head as he noticed movement inside his territory. The powerful horse stamped the ground and then headed for Jamie, trotting at first but quickly picking up speed. Pieces of grass spit up behind him where his hooves butchered the turf.

By the time Becky's feet became unstuck Scott had already sprinted halfway across the yard. Alidor was barreling toward Jamie when Scott reached the fence and vaulted over like an Olympian. Heart pounding, Becky froze as Scott ran toward the stallion, arms waving above his head, shouting, "Whoa, there!"

Nostrils flaring, Alidor diverted his attention from the boy to the man. He stopped in front of Scott, neck extended. Scott leaped backward in time to escape the snap of the Thoroughbred's teeth.

Jamie picked up something in the grass and ran for the fence.

When Scott danced sideways to avoid a second attempt to bite him, the horse changed his approach. He whirled around to present his backside and raised a hind leg. Scott didn't wait around for the kick but made a dash for the fence and leaped over.

Not as gracefully the second time. His boot caught on the top plank and he went sprawling face-first in the grass.

Becky ran forward and dropped to her knees beside him. "Are you okay? Is anything broken?"

He didn't answer. Should she call 9-1-1? She drew breath to shout at Tyler to run inside to the phone when Scott moaned and rolled over onto his back.

"That was kind of a klutzy move, wasn't it?"

Relief flooded through her. She threw herself forward to give him a fierce hug. "That was the best move I've ever seen anyone make."

Embarrassed, she straightened. Scott lay in the grass, looking up at her with an expression of pure astonishment. What must he think of her? Last night he sees her out with her ex-husband, and today she's practically rolling in the grass with him.

She turned to find Jamie and Tyler watching. When she spoke to the older twin, her voice came out sharp. "You are in so much trouble, young man. What in the world were you doing? Don't you know you could have been killed?"

His dark eyes went round and his lower lip quivered. "I saw this." He held it toward her. "I thought it was a man."

She looked at the object in Jamie's hand. A clear glass tube with a red lid. What in the world would make the boy think that was a toy? True, the lid was bright red, and might look the color of the trim on some of his action figures. Maybe if the sun glinted off it just so.

Scott rolled over on his side and sat up with a grunt. He took the object and held it up to the sunlight.

"It's an empty test tube. How'd that get in Alidor's paddock?"

A test tube. She hadn't seen one of those since high school science class. Way back then she'd done experiments, mixing chemicals, looking at specimens under a microscope.

Where had she read about microscopes lately? Seems like she'd seen something in the paper, something about…

Becky's eyes widened. She grabbed Scott's arm. "Do you remember that article we found in Neal's file? The one on cloning?"

His brow creased. "Yeah, so?"

Becky jumped to her feet and ran toward the house. Inside, she flipped through the files, scanning the neatly labeled tabs until she found the one she wanted. She shuffled the papers inside. Where was…there.

When she got back outside, the article clutched in her hand, no one had moved.

"It's right here." She waved the clipping in Scott's face. "It's talking about the first successful horse cloning in the U.S., in Texas."

He looked, but made no move to take it. "Okay. But surely you can't think this has anything to do with Alidor."

A car pulled into the driveway. Becky closed her eyes and dropped her head forward. Christopher's timing was perfect.

The boys raced across the grass toward him. Becky followed more slowly as Scott got to his feet.

Chris got out of the car and leaned against the hood, his arms folded. His eyes bored into hers as she approached. "Having a little romp in the grass, are we?"

Becky looked at the boys, then gave him a stern look. "Christopher, please."

"I just don't like catching my wife with another man."

Anger flared in Becky. "Ex-wife. I know exactly how you feel," she snapped.

At least he had the decency to flush. She set her teeth together until her jaws ached as she helped the boys into the backseat and made sure their seat belts were fastened.

Jamie avoided her eye, probably hoping also to avoid punishment for his stunt. She patted him on the leg and whispered, "We'll talk later."

Straightening, she turned to Christopher. "You will be careful, right?"

"Sure, I will."

She dipped her head, forcing him to lock eyes with her. "No drinking. Not even one beer."

The cocky Christopher-grin twisted his lips. He held up two fingers. "Scout's honor."

"You were never a Boy Scout." She stepped away from the car, her heart wrenching in her chest as he got in and slammed the door. Her babies were about to go on their first visitation with their father without her. *Lord, please, please, please keep them safe!*

"Have them home by six," she called as the car backed out of the driveway.

Christopher waved out the window, and then they were gone.

Her lower lip quivering much as Jamie's had earlier, she turned toward the office. Scott stood by the back door, watching. "You could have gone with them if you wanted. There's nothing pressing going on this afternoon."

He was trying not to look at her, and that suited her fine. If he said anything nice, she might just burst into tears.

She raised her chin. "No, that's okay. It's good for them to be without me every now and then."

"Well." He cleared his throat, then gestured toward the newspaper clipping still clutched in her hand. "About that article."

"Oh." She held it toward him. "I read it when I filed it away. That test tube reminded me of the procedure they describe in there. It says here they take a skin cell sample from the horse, and the DNA is placed into an unfertilized egg that's had the nucleus removed. Then they implant the egg into a fertile mare during breeding session."

Scott's head jerked upright, his gaze fixing on Alidor. "Skin cells? Does it say where on the animal they get them?"

"I don't think so." She looked up at him. "But it *is* breeding season."

He took the article and scanned it. As he neared the end, he shook his head. "It doesn't." He caught her eye. "I've found odd nicks on the ears of a couple of the horses."

The prickling sensation on the back of her neck had nothing to do with the light spring breeze that stirred the leaves above her. "Do you think Neal was cloning the stallions?"

Scott shook his head. "It doesn't make sense. Why would anyone want to clone a Thoroughbred? The Jockey Club won't register cloned foals. They specifically address that in the regulations. Clones can't race, and they can't be bred, so what's the point?"

Becky had no answer for that. "You're right. It doesn't make sense. But I have a feeling it's true."

But Scott kept staring at the article. "Lee Courtney needs to know about this."


"I don't believe it of Neal." Sitting in an armchair, Mr. Courtney removed his reading glasses but continued to stare at the article in his hand.

Becky shifted forward on the elegant sofa cushion and crossed her ankles. They'd closed up the Pasture office an hour early after Scott called Mr. Courtney's secretary and arranged a meeting at his house.

Beside her, Scott tapped the test tube in his palm. "I know it's far-fetched. Nobody would be stupid enough to think they could clone a Thoroughbred."

Mr. Courtney's thick eyebrows rose. "Not as far-fetched as you think. Over in Europe they've made remarkable progress in equine cloning procedures. The Jockey Club is monitoring the situation. Used to be the clones weren't as hardy or as healthy as the originals. I've heard that's changing. Of course, up until now they've experimented on workhorses and pets. But it's only a matter of time before someone tries it on a Thoroughbred." He leaned back in his chair, shaking his head. "I just didn't think about it happening here. Still the Pasture is the perfect place, isn't it?"

Becky thought of the horses they had at the Pasture. Champions, all of them. Millionaires, Neal used to say, because most of them had amassed millions during their racing and breeding careers. "If someone's going to clone a horse," she said slowly, "naturally they'd try for a champion."

Mr. Courtney nodded. "Exactly."

"So you *do* think Haldeman might have been trying to clone the horses," Scott said.

"Not for a minute." Mr. Courtney's chin jutted forward as he fixed a gaze on Scott. "Neal Haldeman had his vices, no doubt, but he loved the industry. He would never do anything to interfere with the natural process of breeding a champion. Never."

Becky leaned forward. "If someone else was trying to collect skin cell specimens from the horses at the Pasture, and if Neal caught them…"

She left the thought unfinished, but judging by their serious expressions, both men followed her logic.

Scott shook his head. "But who would do something so risky? And why? You can't register a clone."

"I don't know why. Maybe just to say they succeeded." Mr. Courtney's lips twisted with disgust. "I can think of only one person who would try something stupid like cloning a Thoroughbred. And he has access to the Pasture, since his property adjoins mine on the back side."

"Nick Stevens?" Becky cast a quick glance toward Scott. Would he mention Nick's wife, Leslie, and her affair with Neal?

Mr. Courtney nodded. "Exactly. He's an upstart, an amateur. He has no respect for the industry, for the breed."

Becky shifted and avoided the older man's glance. That he didn't like Nick, a competitor in the breeding industry, was common knowledge, but to accuse him of this crazy scheme, and maybe even of murder? She didn't believe it.

Scott shook his head. "I still don't understand why. What would he get out of it?"

"Who knows?" The older man stood, a signal that their meeting was over. "I think you should turn this over to the police. Let them sort it out."

Becky got to her feet and took the newspaper clipping Mr. Courtney held out to her. "Thank you for meeting with us on such short notice."

He waved a hand. "Any time. That's what I'm here for. And I was going to call you this afternoon anyway." He shifted his gaze to Scott, a smile tweaking the edges of his mouth. "The board met today. They've authorized me to offer you the position of director of the Pasture on a permanent basis. If you want the job, it's yours."

Becky whirled toward Scott. "That's wonderful news! Congratulations, Scott."

Instead of the wide smile she expected, Scott looked as though he'd just been handed a prison sentence. He stared at the floor in front of him, lips pursed. Didn't he want the job?

"They've decided I'm not disreputable after all?"

Mr. Courtney laughed and clapped him on the back. "They all know that was a misunderstanding. I explained it to them. And several of our donors have been vocal in their support of you. You're the right man for the job."

"I'll have to think about it, Lee." Scott cleared his throat. "I have another offer I'm considering as well."

Ah. So that's what he meant the other day when he said he might not be around much longer. Becky glanced at Mr. Courtney.

The old gentleman didn't seem surprised. "I heard a rumor Francine Buchanan's looking for a new manager over at her place."

Buchanan? Her face went cold as the blood drained away. Scott was going to work for Kaci Buchanan's mother?

"Assistant manager, actually." Scott lifted a shoulder. "But the general manager there is a few years from retirement."

Mr. Courtney watched him a moment, then nodded slowly. "Might be a good opportunity. But don't forget, Zach isn't too many years from retirement himself. I'll be looking for someone to take over Shady Acres before long."

Becky plucked at the hem of her sweater, feeling like an intruder in this conversation. Was it wrong to want Scott to stay at the Pasture when she, herself, was considering leaving? What did it matter that he spent time with Kaci? Becky had no claim on him.

But the thought of Scott with the tall blonde made her green with envy.

Scott flashed a quick smile at Mr. Courtney. "I'll pray about it and let you know next week."

He was silent as they left the house and climbed into the truck. Becky stared out the window as he pulled down the driveway, grasping for something to say. She had no right at all to offer advice about which job he took, but everything in her wanted to scream that he should turn down the Buchanan job and stay at the Pasture.

He broke the silence in the truck as he pulled out onto the road. "I'm going to wait until tomorrow to call the police about Stevens."

She twisted in her seat to face him. "I think Mr. Courtney is right. We should call them now."

One arm extended, the hand draped across the top of the steering wheel, he stared through the windshield as he answered. "I don't think we have enough to make a convincing case. Yet."

Becky narrowed her eyes. "What do you mean, yet?"

"I've been thinking about that guy, Rawlins. Why would Stevens hire him to run the breeding shed when he doesn't know squat? Well, maybe he doesn't know about horses, but maybe he does know about cloning procedures."

"You think Jason is a scientist?" Becky shook her head. The guy didn't look like her idea of a cloning specialist.

Scott shrugged one shoulder. "I don't know what he is, but there's something not right about him. And he's just one more strange circumstance hovering around Nick Stevens."

Becky knew what he meant. "You mean his wife having an affair with the manager of a farm full of retired champion Thoroughbreds?"

Scott nodded. "What if he discovered the affair? If Stevens wanted to get a skin sample from one of the stallions, what better time to do it than when he knew Haldeman was busy with Leslie?

"Okay, so why aren't we calling the police now?"

The truck slowed and Scott's knuckles whitened on the wheel as they neared the driveway of the Pasture. "Because unless we have something other than a suspicion, they won't listen. Nick Stevens is a pretty important guy in this town, no matter what Lee says. They won't do anything on a vague suspicion, and we'll look like alarmists."

The same way they didn't do anything about Mr. Keller. Becky hadn't heard a single word about him being charged for the break-in. "Money talks in this town," she said drily.

"Exactly. But if I get proof, then they'll move."

The truck turned into the driveway, and Becky clutched the seat belt to keep from sliding sideways. "What kind of proof?"

He shoved the shifter into park and turned toward her. "I've been thinking. All that DNA work would need a pretty fancy laboratory. Now, maybe Stevens has connections over at the university or something, but that would be risky. Plus, he's got tons of money. If it were me, I'd build my own laboratory."

Becky's eyes rounded as she followed his train of thought. "His new barn."

Scott smiled. "I want to get a look inside that barn."

# TWENTY-TWO

$B$ecky arrived home to find Chris and the boys pitching a baseball back and forth. Jamie and Tyler ran to hug her when she got out of the car.

"Mommy, you should have seen how far I hit the ball." Tyler's little chest swelled. "Dad said it was a triple for sure."

"And I have a good arm," Jamie informed her. "I might be a pitcher, or maybe a shortstop."

Chris ruffled his hair, laughing. "You'll have to work on catching those line drives, though."

She smiled as she unlocked the house. "With all the practice you're getting, I'll bet you boys will be the stars of your team."

"Yeah!"

When she pushed the door open, the boys tumbled inside. Jamie ran to put his ball glove in the bedroom, but Tyler stopped and turned an inquisitive glance toward his father.

"You coming, Dad?"

Chris shook his head. "I've got to get going, but I'll see you tomorrow, okay?"

"Okay." The boy followed his brother down the hallway at a trot.

"Tomorrow?" She raised an eyebrow at Chris.

"Yeah, I told them we'd all four go to breakfast and then spend the day together. I hope that's okay."

"How did it go?" Becky searched Chris's face. "You didn't have any problems?"

"Nah." Chris's face scrunched. "Well, not at first. After a while they wanted to come home. Kept asking when you'd be here."

Poor Chris. It must be hard to realize your sons aren't comfortable being alone with you. She laid a hand on his arm. "They'll get used to you. Give them time."

He leaned against the doorjamb and looked at her in the old way, the way that made her feel as though he could see all the way inside her.

"Listen, Beck." She ignored a flutter in her stomach. Nobody had called her Beck in more than four years. "I'm leaving early Sunday to get back to Florida. I've got to go to work on Monday. Are you coming with me?"

Was he kidding? She shook her head. "I can't just pick up and go. I have a job, responsibilities here."

Hope flared in his eyes. "Then you are coming eventually?"

Her gaze dropped. "I don't know."

"What's stopping you? We were good together once. We could be again." The twins' arguing voices drifted down the hallway, and he grinned. "We could be even better now. A real family."

"Why, Chris?" She searched his face. "Why do you want me back? I'm not the same person I was. I won't party with you like I used to, and I won't want you to, either. The boys need a positive influence in their lives."

"There's nothing wrong with a little partying every now and then." When she opened her mouth to protest, he laid a finger gently on her lips. "I said a little. Not like before. I've grown up, Beck. I'm ready to be a father, and a husband."

Her mouth went completely dry. Never in her wildest dreams did she expect to hear Christopher talking like this. "I'm a Christian now," she blurted. "I'm going to raise the boys in church."

He returned her gaze without flinching. "I can deal with that." A corner of his mouth lifted. "You never know. Maybe I'll even come with you every now and then. On special occasions."

Did he mean it? Was Christopher really ready to settle down? And would he really consider coming to church with her? He looked sincere. Once upon a time, years ago, she would have given anything to hear him say he wanted to be a father to the boys and a husband to her.

But now…

"I'll think about it."

"Well, you might want to hurry." He leaned forward, until his face was inches from hers. "We have a lot of catching up to do."

She stepped back quickly, out of kissing range. She wasn't ready for that yet.

His eyes danced with humor as he straightened. "I'll see you at nine in the morning."

"I don't know, Daddy." She rinsed milk residue out of a plastic cup and set it in the top rack of the dishwasher. "He seems sincere."

"I can't believe I'm hearing you. This is the guy who cheated on you when you were pregnant with his sons. Maybe you've forgotten all the tears you cried on my shoulder, but I sure haven't."

A lively song from a children's DVD sounded from the other room, punctuated by childish giggles. She switched the phone to the other shoulder.

"I haven't forgotten, but things are different now. I'm more mature, for one thing."

"One mature person can't support a marriage on her own."

"I know that."

The last supper dish loaded in the dishwasher, she wet a dishrag to wipe the table.

Daddy's voice lost its angry edge. He became serious. "Becky, what's going on? There's something you're not telling me, something more than just wanting a father for Tyler and Jamie. What's pushing you back to this guy?"

She tossed the dishrag into the sink and dropped into a kitchen chair. "Daddy, I've made so many mistakes. I wonder sometimes if this is God's way of giving me a chance to make things right."

"Hold on. You think *God* sent that lowlife back to you?"

"Have you ever considered that maybe I'm the only way He will ever get through to Chris?" Elbow on the table, she leaned her forehead on her fingers and massaged a dull ache behind her eyes. "I keep remembering that verse that says a believing wife can win her husband."

A long pause. "So that's what this is all about. You think you sinned when you divorced, and now you've got to make it up to God by going back to the guy."

Becky cringed at the heavy sarcasm in his voice. Or maybe it wasn't his tone, but the fact that he had just hit at the heart of her feelings. She hadn't thought it through, but that's exactly what she felt. She had to make it up, not only to God but also to her boys.

"Listen, Becky. I could pull out the Bible to try to

convince you that you're making a fool-headed mistake. The one about not being unequally yoked comes to mind. I'm no Bible scholar, but I'll bet I could find more.

"The point is this. You don't fix past mistakes with new ones. And going back to Christopher Dennison would be a colossal mistake for you and the twins."

"You don't know that." She straightened and placed her hand on the table. "You haven't talked to him in almost five years."

"Maybe I don't know the reasons, but I feel it in my bones." He stopped, then went on more gently. "That's it, sweetheart. I feel it, and I think you do, too. You know I'm not real smart when it comes to the Bible, but one thing I do know. God tells us what to do. The trick is learning how to ignore ourselves and listen to him. I just don't think you're listening hard enough."

A hush stole over the kitchen. Becky went still. From the other room, the sound blared from the television as though from a great distance. Daddy's words had the ring of truth. She'd been so busy feeling guilty, she hadn't prayed about this situation with Chris. Or, she realized with a sudden rush of emotion, about her relationship with Scott. She'd assumed she knew the answers, but she'd never asked the questions. How could she possibly make the right decision if she hadn't even taken the time to pray?

Her grip on the phone relaxed until it was almost a caress. "Thanks, Daddy. I know what I need to do now."

Dressed in black, Scott hugged as close to the fencerow as he could. He'd left his truck over at the Pasture and snuck onto the Stevenses' property through the back part of Shady Acres. Nick and Leslie's house, tucked in a back corner at the end of a long, smooth driveway, glowed like a light-house in a storm, a landmark on the otherwise dark farm.

Feeling like a criminal, he nearly jumped out of his skin when a dark horse in the paddock beside him whinnied softly.

"Shh, there now." He pitched his voice low, soothing. "Nothing to worry about. I'll be in and out in no time."

Wispy clouds moved across a fingernail moon, throwing strange shadows on the whitewashed side of the new barn. Thoroughbred breeders liked to erect fancy barns, and this was one of the better-built ones Scott had seen. Sturdy construction, thick siding, neatly trimmed windows with elaborately designed shutters. Nicer by far than the plain little cottage he rented from Lee Courtney. And about ten times the size. Situated as it was on the northernmost edge of the farm's cleared land, and backing up to a thick copse of trees, this out-of-the-way location was the perfect place to hide a laboratory.

He came to the place where he had to leave the sparse cover of the fenced pasture and cross a packed dirt road to approach the barn. A big cloud raced across the night sky, blown by a spring breeze, and Scott waited until it covered the moon. In the resulting darkness, he dashed across the road and into the deep shadows on the far side of the building.

He peeked around the corner. Not a movement anywhere. Light shone through windows up at the Stevenses' home about a hundred yards distant, far enough away that he couldn't see anything through them. If anyone happened to be looking out, hopefully they couldn't see this far, either.

He figured there'd be another door in the rear, like the barn at the Pasture. Sure enough, there was an entrance on this side. Probably one on the opposite side, as well, the one that faced the house. Hopefully it wouldn't be locked.

When he pushed, it moved beneath his hand. It was not latched. Ready to dart into the trees at the first sound or sight of movement, he slid the door open inch by painstaking inch. Just enough to slip through.

Inside, the building was like a cave. His sneaker squeaked on the floor, the sound echoing with a hollow ring in the otherwise silent interior. The place smelled fresh, like new paint and raw timber. He shut his eyes tight, trying to adjust them to the pitch black, then opened them again. Still too dark to see anything. Well, at least the windows were all shuttered. Nobody would see his flashlight.

He pulled a slim penlight out of his back pocket. Heart thundering, he twisted the cap.

Amazing what a dim light could do in a dark place. He aimed the narrow beam toward the front of the barn, noted a half-dozen empty stalls. Nothing in that direction. Looked like any other horse barn.

He pointed toward the rear, and his pulse quickened. The entire back fourth of the barn was walled off. A small window punctuated the left of the partition, shuttered from the other side. On the right, a door. Shut.

Scott moved as silently as he could, each step placed with careful precision. The door was sure to be locked. If it was, he couldn't bring himself to break in. Maybe the shutter on the window wasn't latched and he could push it in enough to see.

He grabbed the doorknob and twisted.

It turned. Not locked.

He eased it open a crack and pointed the flashlight inside, expecting to see shiny metal surfaces and microscopes. Instead, the beam illuminated an ordinary bedroom. A single bed stood in one corner, and beside it, a four-drawer dresser with a small television set on the top. Lining the back wall were a small table with two chairs, a half-sized refrigerator and a cabinet with a microwave oven. Beside the dresser a door stood open and he glimpsed the corner of a toilet.

In the next instant, his dark-accustomed eyes were blinded by a flood of bright light. His penlight clattered to the floor.

A voice echoed in the empty barn behind him. "I have a gun pointed at your back. If you move an inch, I'll shoot you."

# TWENTY-THREE

Scott went statue-still, hand over his eyes. The police? But then the voice registered, and he knew who stood behind him. If only it *was* the police!

"Turn around slowly. Keep those hands where I can see them."

He did as he was told. "Listen, I know this looks bad. I can explain."

Nicholas Stevens didn't look receptive to his explanations. His glower deepened when he recognized Scott, and he gripped the shotgun tighter to his side.

"Lewis. I should have known. I can smell Lee Courtney's stink all the way over here."

"You've got it wrong, Stevens. Lee doesn't have any idea I'm here."

Scott tried to keep his gaze locked on Nick's face, but it kept sliding downward like metal to a magnet. He'd never had the barrel of a gun pointed in his direction. Not a good feeling.

Nick's eyelids narrowed. "I don't believe you. Courtney and all those other blue bloods have had it in for me since Leslie and I bred our first foal. I don't know what he sent you over here to do, but I think I'd better call the police and let them figure it out."

"Honest, Nick." Scott kept his hands in front of him, in full sight. "I came on my own. I wasn't planning to do anything bad. I wanted to get a look inside your barn, that's all."

The barrel dropped a fraction. "You have about thirty seconds to explain why, and it'd better be good."

Scott wished he had good explanation. At the moment, a horse cloning scheme sounded about as far-fetched as little green men from Mars.

"Well, it's kind of strange, really." He gave a laugh, at which Nick's scowl only deepened. "See, we've found a couple of things over at the Pasture that led us to believe Haldeman might have been involved in an experiment." Yeah, an experiment. That sounded good. "But it would have required a scientific laboratory." He cleared his throat. "I, uh, got to thinking about this brand-new barn, and, well, here I am."

"You thought I had a laboratory in my barn?" The barrel slipped farther as lines creased Nick's brow. "What kind of laboratory?"

"It gets a little crazy here." Scott tried to keep his gaze straight. "A horse cloning laboratory."

Nick's stare became incredulous. "You think I'm cloning horses?"

"It wouldn't have occurred to me at all, except I met your new shed manager the other day. Frankly, he didn't seem to have much experience. Made me a little suspicious."

His lips twisted. "Well, you got that right, anyway. He doesn't know the first thing about horses. But he's Leslie's kid brother, and she insisted on hiring him."

Scott rocked back on his heels. Leslie's brother? "So he's not a scientist?"

Nick's laughter echoed off the vaulted ceiling. "Scientist? He's a high school dropout. Hasn't held a job longer than six months in his life." He nodded toward the room behind Scott. "Leslie had that apartment put in for him, and moved him here from Phoenix. Against my better judgment, but she's softhearted. Said she'd keep an eye on him. She's more involved in the day-to-day operations of the place than I am, so I agreed."

Never in his life had Scott felt more like an idiot than he did at this moment. "Listen, Nick, I'm sorry. I let my imagination get the better of me. I shouldn't have."

Nick studied him for a long moment, then finally shouldered the shotgun with a shrug. "It's all right. I can't say I like you sneaking around my farm in the middle of the night, but I guess since Haldeman's death we're all a little jumpy."

Tension melted out of Scott's shoulders as the menace of the shotgun was removed. "Thanks. You're more understanding than I deserve."

Nick cocked his head. "Do you really think Haldeman was cloning horses?" His eyes widened. "Man, some of those old stallions over there were top-notch in their day."

Scott nodded. "I know. But if he was, I don't know how he did it. He had to be working with someone."

Nick's right hand went up, palm facing Scott. "Not me. You can search every barn on my farm if you want. You won't find a laboratory anywhere." He grinned, which went a long way toward taking the edge off Scott's guilt.

Scott shook his head. "Thanks, but I'll take your word on that. I think I'll let the police handle it from here."

"Sounds like a good idea to me."

Nick turned, indicating that Scott should precede him out of the barn. Scott did, but kept his eye on the shotgun, just in case.

Nick noticed him staring at it. He hefted it in his hand and laughed. "It's not loaded. I was standing outside having a smoke when I saw you cross the road. I grabbed it out of my pickup, but forgot to get the shells out of the glove compartment."

Scott grinned. "Now you tell me."

"I'm hungry, Mommy. When will he get here?" Tyler didn't normally whine, so his nasally tone told Becky he was more anxious than hungry.

When Chris didn't show up by ten, she'd fed the boys cereal. She glanced at the clock. Almost twelve-thirty. And still no answer in his motel room. For the fiftieth time she wished she'd asked who he was meeting last night.

"I don't know, sweetheart. Do you want a peanut butter sandwich?"

His head drooped. "No."

Jamie sat on the couch, watching television without a word. Occasionally he looked over his shoulder, out the window toward the driveway. His sad little frown nearly broke her heart. She'd gone through this countless times during the last months of her marriage. She'd grown accustomed to hours of gut-wrenching worry, wondering whether she should call the hospital emergency room to see if Chris had been in an accident.

But she wasn't five years old. Becky's teeth clenched. Chris had better have a good explanation for disappointing the boys.

She picked up the remote control and pressed the Off button. Neither twin protested, an indication of how anxious they were.

"Boys, listen to me." She waited until both sets of eyes

were fixed on her. "I know you're worried about your daddy. Do you remember what we do when we're upset about something?"

Jamie raised a tentative hand as though he was in school, and Becky hid a smile.

"We pray?" he asked.

She nodded. "That's right. Do you want me to pray with you now?"

"Okay."

Tyler slipped off the couch to his knees, Jamie right behind him. They placed their arms on the cushion, and clasped their hands together like they did every night before she tucked them in bed. Eyes closed, their dark heads dropped forward.

Her heart twisting in her chest, Becky joined her boys on the floor and bowed her head.

"Dear Lord, Jamie and Tyler are worried because they don't know where their daddy is." She cracked an eyelid open and saw Jamie nod in agreement. "But You know where he is, because You know everything. So we ask You to watch over him and keep him safe."

"And don't let him be in a wreck," said Jamie.

"And let him get here soon," Tyler added.

"And most of all," Becky continued, "let him know how much You love him. In Jesus' Name, Amen."

"Amen," they chorused.

Smiles lit their eyes as they both threw arms around her. Hugging them for all she was worth, Becky added a silent prayer of her own. *And please guard their hearts, Lord. I can't stand to see them disappointed.*

"There he is!" Tyler leaped up and ran to the front door, his brother a half second behind him.

Becky stood at the window, watching as the twins dashed across the yard to the car. Chris got out slowly and closed the door with exaggerated care. Dark glasses obscured his eyes, but even across the distance she saw his grimace as Tyler grabbed his arm.

How many times had she seen him move like that? About a million. He was hungover.

Opening the door, Becky stepped out onto the front porch. "Boys, you go on inside. I want to talk to your father for a minute."

Strangely subdued, Tyler obeyed without arguing. Jamie looked up at Chris once, then followed his brother past her and into the house.

Chris sank onto the concrete steps and lowered his head to his hands. "I gotta siddown a minute."

The back of his hair had an unbrushed tangle, ends hanging limply down past the collar of his T-shirt. Though fury at his disregard for his sons' feelings brought angry words to the tip of her tongue, she was surprised to feel the stirrings of compassion. He looked like a miserable wretch.

She sat down beside him, careful to keep space between them. The smell of sour beer wrinkled her nose. Whether it emanated from his clothes or oozed from his pores, she couldn't tell.

"You look terrible."

"I feel worse." He spoke barely above a whisper.

"Did you have a good time?" Her voice dripped sarcasm which she doubted he heard.

A pain-filled smile lifted the edges of his lips. "As far as I can remember."

Becky shook her head. Thank the Lord she had outgrown that behavior. Maybe one day Chris would, too.

"I ought to lecture you about disappointing your sons." He didn't react at all, and she continued. "But I'll save that for when you're completely sober. In the meantime, I want to tell you that I've made a decision."

He lifted the corner of one hand and tilted his head to peer at her through a bloodshot eye from the side of his sunglasses. "I can tell from your expression. You're staying here, aren't you?"

She nodded. "I'm sorry, Chris. I'll do whatever I can to make sure you have a good relationship with Tyler and Jamie." She softened her voice. "But the fact is, I don't love you. Marrying you again would be just one more big mistake. I'm sorry."

He bent double, his head hanging between his knees. For a moment he didn't say anything. Then he raised his head. "Yeah, well, I figured that from the way you were looking at your boss the other night."

A blush heated her cheeks, but she kept her mouth shut. She didn't owe him anything, including an explanation.

Chris heaved himself to his feet, groaning. "I gotta go. I need a little hair of the dog. Tell the boys I'll call 'em later."

Becky watched him lurch toward his car. Though Jamie and Tyler would be heartbroken, that was much better than letting them spend time around their father in this shape.

As he slid behind the wheel, she stood. Two little faces, so much like Chris's but fresh and clean and unpolluted by the harsh life he'd lived, watched her anxiously from the window. She forced a smile, fighting against a sadness that threatened to make her cry. He was their father. As their mother, she always would make sure they were safe, but she couldn't shield them from him completely. He probably loved them as much as he was able, but they'd just have to get used to being disappointed by him.

Starting now.

Scott looked at the sore on Kiri's flank. Doc Matthews had said it wasn't ringworm, and he put some ointment on it, but the place hadn't cleared up. In fact, it looked worse, as if it had become infected.

Doc, like most everyone who had anything to do with horses, was at Keeneland this last Saturday of the spring races. No chance of getting him out here until Monday.

But they kept some antibiotic ointment over in the Shady Acres farm office. He could use that for a day or two. Sure wouldn't hurt, and he had to do something.

"Come on, Sam." He whistled for the yellow Lab. "Let's go across the road."

A lone stable boy occupied the Shady Acres barn, seated at a bench in the tack room. Scott heard the tinny notes and rhythmic thump of bass from his headphones, smelled the leather cleaner on the rag he rubbed over a saddle. He jumped like a nervous cat when Scott tapped him on the shoulder.

He jerked the earphones off his head. "Mr. Lewis, you scared the daylights out of me."

Scott grinned and nodded toward his iPod. "You'll go deaf if you're not careful, Ben."

Ben rolled his eyes. "You sound like my mother."

Laughing, Scott left him to finish listening to his song and headed toward the office.

His keys jangled as he unlocked the windowed office door. Inside, the surface of the desk was littered with files and untidy stacks of paperwork. He crossed to the metal cabinet along the back row and slid the door open. Inside, he scanned across the various bottles and tubes, looking for the one he wanted.

Not here. Maybe Shady Acres was out of the antibiotic ointment, too.

One more place to look. The junk drawer. The bottom desk drawer served as repository for everything that either didn't have a permanent storage place, or that someone didn't want to take the time to put away. Scott sat in the rolling chair and yanked on the handle.

Locked. That was odd. They never bothered to lock the desk drawers, because the office stayed locked whenever nobody was in it. Scott sorted through the keys on his ring, grasping the smallest one between his fingers. He slipped it into the lock and opened the drawer.

What a mess. It was even more full than when he last looked. He pawed through a variety of stuff, pushing aside a stapler, a ball of metal wire, a roll of duct tape. Where was that tube of ointment?

He'd just about decided he was out of luck when he grabbed a grooming cloth and shoved it to the front of the pile. It unrolled as it moved, uncovering an item that had been wrapped inside.

Scott's hand halted. He stared. Blood roared in his ears in rhythm with his pulse.

A hoof pick.

Barely breathing, Scott gawked at the tool as his mind raced. Maybe there was a plausible explanation for a hoof pick to be in the junk drawer. Even though it should be in the tack room with the rest of the grooming equipment. Maybe it was broken or something.

Careful not to touch it, Scott dropped the cloth over the red plastic handle and picked it up. It wasn't broken. He examined the metal hook closely, almost afraid to find the telltale signs of blood. It was clean, thank goodness. A little too clean, maybe? Shouldn't there be dirt or something on it?

*Stop it. The boys keep the equipment clean.*

Pulse pounding, he set the tool on the desk. Was this the instrument of Neal Haldeman's demise?

Only one other person had keys to this desk. Zach Garrett.

Scott leaned back in the chair, unable to tear his gaze from the hoof pick. No. He refused to believe it. Zach had been nothing but kind to him since he came to Shady Acres. They didn't have a lot in common outside of the horses, but he was a nice guy. Not a killer.

Cold fingers slid up his spine, and the hair on his arms rose. Zach had wanted the temporary job over at the Pasture. He'd been irritated when Lee gave it to Scott. Why would he be eager to walk away from the Shady Acres manager position with the responsibility and staff and all the prestige that went with it?

Was Zach in cahoots with Haldeman to clone the stallions?

No. This had to be another misunderstanding, just like the one with Nick Sanders. There had to be an explanation.

And Scott wanted—no needed—to hear it.

# TWENTY-FOUR

The ringing of the telephone interrupted their movie.

"I'll get it!" Tyler jumped up from the living room floor and ran for the phone in the kitchen.

"Want me to pause it, Mommy?" Jamie, in control of the remote tonight, held an eager finger above the button.

"Sure."

Becky glanced at the wall clock. A few minutes past six-thirty. About time Chris called. The boys had waited all afternoon. In a blatant effort to soothe their aching feelings, Becky had splurged on a supper of junk food and a movie rental.

She heard Tyler's high-pitched, "Hello?" from the kitchen, followed by a pause. "Hi, Mr. Lewis. I'll get Mommy."

Scott calling her? A sudden attack of nerves made her want to giggle, but she bit it back. She'd itched all day long to call him, to tell him about her decision. But what would he think? That she was chasing him? That she was man-hungry? Images of the tall, gorgeous Kaci Buchanan taunted her and kept her from picking up the phone.

But now he was calling her.

"Go ahead and press Play," she told Jamie. "I'll catch up with the movie in a minute."

She intercepted Tyler in the doorway and took the phone from him. He scooted past her, grabbed a handful of chips from the bag on the coffee table and returned to his place on the floor in front of the television.

"Hello?"

"Becky, it's Scott." His voice sounded odd, tight.

"What's wrong?"

"Nothing. I don't know. I found something."

She sank into a chair, listening with growing disbelief as he described his discovery in the office at Shady Acres.

"So you called the police, right?" Her voice came out in a squeak, and she lowered it. "Please tell me you called the police."

"Not yet. I have to talk to him, Becky. I've been falsely accused before, and I won't do that to anyone else. I've worked with Zach for almost a year now, and I owe him that."

"You don't owe him a thing if he *killed Neal*." She hissed the last words, glancing toward the doorway to make sure the twins were still in the living room. "And don't forget that bookie. Two people are dead, Scott. If he's responsible, he might come after you, too."

"That's why I called you. I don't want to go over there without someone knowing where I am. I'm sorry to pull you into this, but I didn't think I should call Lee. Zach might have a perfectly logical explanation for that hoof pick, and then he won't thank me for calling his boss."

Her insides clenched into a knot. She wanted to scream at him, would have, if the boys hadn't been in the other room. "Scott, this is a mistake." She let a note of unabashed pleading saturate her tone. "Please call the police."

He ignored her. "It's six-thirty now. I'm at my house,

and I can see his place from here. It's dark. I know he went to Keeneland today, but he should be home soon. I want you to do me a favor." He paused. "If you don't hear from me by eight o'clock, call the police."

His tone chilled her to the bone. "Scott, I'm afraid. Please don't do this."

"I'll be fine. Promise me you won't call the cops before eight, okay?"

She hesitated. "I don't think—"

"Please, Becky. I'm counting on you."

She couldn't think straight. Her gut screamed *No,* but he was counting on her. She couldn't deny him. She heaved a loud sigh into the phone, another indication to him that she was going against her better judgment. "Okay, I promise not to call the police until eight o'clock. But the moment that second hand hits—"

"You won't have to. I'll be in touch before then." Relief made his voice sound almost normal. "One other thing. Say a prayer for me, okay?"

Her hand trembled so violently the phone slipped away from her ear. "I will. Please be careful."

The line went dead. Becky sat at the kitchen table, her heart pounding. He should not do this alone. If Zach Garrett killed Neal and that bookie, he was a dangerous man. Scott was too trusting. He needed someone else with him, someone to make him see reason. If only she had a babysitter she could leave the boys with on short notice.

After Tuesday night, she wouldn't dare ask Amber. What about…

No. She would *not* call Chris. He'd said something about "hair of the dog," which meant he was probably drunk again tonight.

Her hands balled into fists, and she pounded on the table. Oh, how she hated this helpless feeling!

*Lord, please keep Scott safe.*

The doorbell rang. Becky's teeth clamped together, her jaw tightening with frustration. She did not have the patience to deal with Christopher tonight. And if he thought he was going to come around the boys if he'd been drinking, he had another think coming. She'd just have to send him away, that's all. Tyler and Jamie wouldn't understand, but—

Jamie's excited voice pierced the air. "Grandpa!"

Becky's head jerked upward. Daddy, here?

She leaped up from the chair and ran into the living room. Each twin had hold of one of Daddy's hands, and both hopped like overinflated basketballs, squealing their excitement. Becky threw her arms around her father's neck and hugged for all she was worth.

"I'm so glad to see you." Her voice came out choked. She pulled back and looked at him through pools of tears. "What are you doing here?"

He gave her a stern look. "I caught a 6:00 a.m. flight out of LAX, and it cost me a fortune. I'm here to make sure you don't repeat the biggest mistake of your life."

She hugged him again, laughing. "Thank you. Oh, thank you, Daddy." She straightened. "And you're just in time. I desperately need a babysitter!"


Becky pulled her car into the dirt driveway behind Scott's pickup. She cut the engine and sat with her hands clutching the steering wheel. A chorus of crickets sang a peaceful counterpoint to her twanging nerves. When Scott saw her on his front stoop, he'd think she was no better than

Kaci, blatantly chasing after him. Either that, or he'd be irritated with her.

Too bad. There was no way she intended to let him face a possible killer alone. Steeling herself, she dropped her keys in her purse and stepped out into the cool night air.

The door jerked open when she raised her hand to knock. Judging by the annoyance on his face, he'd chosen the second reaction.

"What are you doing here?" His gaze searched the car behind her. "You didn't bring the boys, did you?"

"Of course not." She drew herself up. "I came to help you. You can't confront Zach by yourself."

The cleft in his chin deepened as his lips tightened. "I certainly can, and I will."

"Scott, be reasonable." Becky adjusted the purse strap on her shoulder. "If there are two of us, he's less likely to try anything."

The next instant, Becky found herself jerked roughly through the door. Scott's fingers bit into her arm as he pulled her to one side and slammed the door shut. He released her, crossed to a window and pulled back a curtain to peek through it.

"He's home. I don't want him to see you."

She couldn't help looking around the tiny room curiously even as she asked, "Why not?" A plain three-cushion sofa, a coffee table and a small television on a cheap metal stand were the only furnishings. Very sparse. Very male.

Scott wasn't watching her. He had his eye up to the crack in the curtains and spoke without turning. "Because if it turns out he's responsible for Haldeman's death, I'd just as soon he not know you're involved." He whirled to face her. "I want you to go home."

She folded her arms and said, "Not a chance."

"But who will call the police if something happens to me?" His stare became suspicious. "You didn't call them before you came, did you?"

Becky returned his stare. "Of course not. I promised, didn't I?"

He peeked out the window. "He's leaving again." The irritated look he turned her way would have made her flinch if she hadn't been trying so hard to look stubborn. "I'm going to miss my chance to talk to him."

An idea sparked. "Let's follow him. Maybe he's going to grab a bite to eat or something. It'll be much safer if you confront him in a public place."

Scott's forehead wrinkled as he considered her suggestion. "Well…"

"Come on!" She grabbed his arm and pulled him toward the door. "He'll get away from us if we don't hurry. I'll drive."

Scott jerked his arm away. "Why should you drive?"

She smiled sweetly. "Because I'm parked behind you."

Scott's fingers cramped from his tight grip on the armrest of Becky's car. "He turned right. Past that white truck."

She took her gaze off the road to glance his way. "I saw him."

He had to admit, she'd done a good job of following Zach's car on the fifteen-minute drive to Lexington, never losing sight of his taillights, but staying far enough back that he wouldn't notice. Once they hit the city limits they got a little closer. But instead of going to a restaurant, as Scott hoped, Zach seemed to be going to someone's house. The car was winding through the quiet streets of a sprawling neighborhood. Not a lot of traffic here to hide them.

"There." His finger left a smudge on the windshield. "He pulled into a driveway. Don't get close to the house."

"I won't."

Becky pulled the car over to the side of the road and cut the lights. Enough cars were parked up and down this residential street that theirs should go unnoticed. They watched as Zach got out of his car and went inside the house without knocking.

"I can't follow him in there. What if he's on a date or something?" Scott's hands knotted into fists. "If you hadn't showed up, I could have confronted him at home, before he took off again."

Becky caught him in a sideways look. "If you hadn't been so mule-headed about talking to him, the police would be doing this instead of us."

He turned away from her piercing gaze. Unexpectedly, his lips twitched. They were snapping at each other like old friends. He swallowed convulsively. Or sweethearts. His smile faded. Which they definitely were not.

He unclipped the cell phone from his belt. "As long as we're here, I'm going to sneak up there and have a look through the back windows."

Her head jerked upward, and her eyes searched his face. "Why in the world would you do that?"

Scott lifted a shoulder. "Call it a hunch. If Zach was involved with Haldeman in a cloning scheme, there's still the matter of the laboratory. Where better to hide it than in the middle of suburbia?"

Her eyes widened as his logic sank in. Then her chin lifted in that stubborn pose he was getting accustomed to seeing. "Then I think we should call—"

"The police. I know." He handed her the cell phone.

"If I'm not back in ten minutes, that's exactly what I want you to do."

He didn't wait to hear her arguments, but unsnapped his seat belt with one hand as he opened the door with the other. He slipped out, crouching, and closed the door as quickly and quietly as he could. The light inside had only been on for a few seconds. Hopefully, not long enough for anyone to notice.

Not that there was anyone to see. The streets were void of movement, though light illuminated the windows of most of the single-story homes that lined both sides of the street. Scott walked down the sidewalk with his arms swinging at his sides. If anybody happened to glance outside, he'd look as if he was just out for a casual stroll.

When he neared the house into which Zach had disappeared, he bent low and darted through the grass and into the side yard. Thankfully, there was no fence. Nor were there any windows on this side of the home, except for a single small one high up, probably in a bathroom. He leaned against the brick and willed his breath to remain even. If he'd known he was going to be sneaking around in the dark, he would have worn his black jeans and shirt.

There was a front window, but no shrubberies or anything else to give him cover. His best bet was to sneak around to the back and hope he could see something from there.

Placing each foot with exaggerated care, he crept along the side of the house. A peek around the corner showed no sign of movement. A privacy fence encased the yard behind this one, so he couldn't be seen from that direction. There was no fence on either side, but there was no sign of anyone there, either.

Four windows on the back of the house. The far two

were dark. Bent double, he slunk toward the first one, through which a bright light shone. With extra caution, he inched upward and looked inside.

A kitchen. Not a very clean one, either. The sink held a load of dirty dishes, and a couple more stacks littered the counter beside it. The stove, too, had pots and pans on it. In the corner, a garbage can overflowed.

Nothing moved inside. Scott strained his ears for any sound from within the house. A dog barked a few houses away, but from inside, nothing. Where was Zach, and why wasn't he talking to whoever lived here?

He moved on to the back door. The handle didn't budge. Probably a good thing. He might have been tempted to sneak inside if it had. The window in the door was covered on the inside with a curtain through which he could see nothing.

The other two windows looked in on empty rooms. Though they were dark, his eyes had adjusted enough that he could see there wasn't a stick of furniture in either one. And the doors were closed, so he couldn't see anything beyond them, either.

He sagged against the wall, disappointed. He'd hoped to find something to justify this harebrained jaunt, so he didn't look like a complete fool in Becky's eyes. Which was stupid, of course. What did it matter what Becky thought? She was going back to her husband.

She was probably right, and they should just call the police. But what if he accused his boss and friend of killing someone, and it turned out the hoof pick he found wasn't the murder weapon after all?

He headed back the way he had come. Maybe he could call Trooper Whitley or Detective Foster and tip them off that he'd found it, and they wouldn't have to tell Zach where they heard it from.

A sound halted him. Someone was coming around the corner. His glance circled the yard frantically, looking for cover.

A moment later, all thoughts of hiding fled. Two familiar figures stepped into the backyard, one with an expression of pure terror on her face. Becky.

In the next instant he realized why. The other figure, walking behind her, was none other than his boss, Zach Garrett. And he held a gun to Becky's head.

# TWENTY-FIVE

Becky looked at Scott's face and saw her fear mirrored there. Zach's grip on her arm didn't hurt, but she imagined her skin burned where his fingers touched. He was a murderer, a cold-blooded killer. The barrel of the gun bumped the back of her head when he jerked her to a stop.

What if she screamed? Surely someone in one of these houses would come to investigate. But he might shoot her or Scott in the meantime.

"I think we'd better go inside." She felt Zach's breath on the crown of her head.

Scott's gaze was fixed on a point behind Becky. On Zach. "It's locked."

At that moment, the back door opened. Afraid to move her head, she stared straight ahead at Scott, but from the corner of her eye saw a thin man shove the door outward and step back inside.

She heard the smile in Zach's voice. "Not anymore. You first."

Scott locked eyes with her for an instant. Becky saw no hope in them at all, and an answering dread welled up in her. If she died, what would happen to Tyler and Jamie?

Would Christopher get custody of them? *No, Lord! Don't let that happen.*

Scott walked up the three concrete steps and into the house. Zach pushed her forward into a filthy kitchen. The smell of rotting food, probably coming from an overflowing trash can in the corner, assaulted her nostrils.

"You really should clean the place every now and then, Tenney." The gun barrel appeared in her peripheral vision as Zach used it to gesture toward a doorway to the right. "Down there, Scott."

The thin man's head jerked nervously toward Zach. "Perhaps you shouldn't take them below." He spoke in a high-pitched, nasally British accent.

"Can't leave them up here. You never know who's sneaking around, peeking through the windows." His laughter sent a shiver up Becky's spine.

Scott went through the doorway and down a set of narrow stairs. She followed, Zach on her heels.

"Go on in that room on the right," Zach instructed. "Might as well see what you came to see."

She followed Scott through a doorway. The room on the other side was not large, but had been refinished with a white-tiled floor and white walls. A long counter, spotlessly clean, took up most of the floor space in the center. Its surface was covered with equipment. The only thing Becky could identify was a microscope, but it had extra stuff attached to it that she'd never seen. Along the far wall was another counter, and atop this one was a machine that looked like a convection oven, with a digital panel on the front.

Zach released her, and she stepped up beside Scott, close enough to draw a scant amount of comfort from contact with his arm. His tight lips cracked in a brief smile that was really more of a grimace. She bit back her rising panic.

"You two stand over there." Zach pointed with his gun toward a corner, and with the other hand flipped open a cell phone. He punched a couple of buttons, then lifted it to his ear. "You on your way?" He nodded. "Good. We have company. Looks like you were right."

As he pocketed the cell phone, Scott stepped in front of her. "Let Becky go, Zach. She'll keep quiet. You have my word."

Zach's smile chilled her to the bone. "I'll wait for my partner. Then we'll decide what to do with both of you."

"Partner?" Becky's voice wavered, and she swallowed. "You mean Neal wasn't your partner?"

"Haldeman?" A humorless blast of laughter lifted his chest. "We tried. He wouldn't have a thing to do with us. Kept going on about the purity of the breeding process. It would have been easier with his help, but we've done okay in spite of him."

"They why did you kill him?"

Becky glanced up at Scott. How could he sound so calm with a gun pointed at his chest?

Zach shrugged. "I didn't mean to. It was an accident."

"You *accidentally* ripped his throat out with a hoof pick?"

Zach's features tightened. Becky put a hand on Scott's arm and squeezed a warning. *Don't antagonize the man with the gun!*

"He was on to us but he couldn't prove anything. Until he caught me in Alidor's paddock. Or," he corrected, "running out of Alidor's paddock. That horse is the meanest, orneriest stallion I ever met."

Ah. Now Jamie's discovery made sense. "You dropped a test tube in there while trying to get a skin cell sample from him."

Zach's gaze slid to her. "Found that, did you? Tenney dropped it, the fool. Didn't tell me until yesterday, though."

Becky glanced toward the stairs that led to the first floor. "Tenney's a scientist?"

Zach smiled. "You catch on quick, don't you? Yeah, he's a scientist. A cloning specialist."

"Why, Zach?" Scott's question sounded sincere as he looked at the older man. "You can't clone a Thoroughbred."

"Oh, but we can. Have, in fact. Twice. One mare's already pregnant with our first success, Dark Diego. And see that over there?" He pointed toward the ovenlike apparatus. "In there is the clone of Samson's Secret, all ready to be implanted."

Becky glanced around the room. There were no windows, no doors except the one they came in. No way out. And no way for anyone to see in, either. With Tenney keeping watch upstairs, no chance of a rescue.

"And then what?" Scott asked. "What are you going to do with a clone? You can't register it."

Zach sneered. "Sure you can. All you have to do is submit a Live Foal Report to the Jockey Club."

Scott's arm twitched. "You can't fake the DNA report."

Zach laughed. "I thought you were smarter than that, Scott. Think about it. In December, two foals will be born. One will be the clone of Dark Diego. The other was bred the regular way, from a mare and stallion the same color as Diego, and with similar markings. Their mating has been duly recorded. The hair we send to the lab for DNA testing will be from the second foal. But the pictures the Jockey Club gets with the Live Foal Report will be from the clone."

The muscles in Scott's jaw bunched before he spoke. "It won't work. Clones aren't as healthy as the original, so it will never win a race."

"Maybe not, but they might surprise you." The sound of a door slamming, followed by the low hum of Tenney's British accent drifted to them from upstairs. Zach continued. "Besides, racing isn't where the real money is made. You know yourself all the winners Alidor has sired. Over thirty-eight million earned by his offspring. Runners bred by his clone could do that, maybe even more."

"You can't breed a clone." Frustration seeped into Scott's voice, and his fist tightened. "The DNA of those foals won't match the Jockey Club's records, unless you forge them, too. You'll have to breed another true foal for every clone, and keep faking the reports. You'll get caught!"

Becky dug her fingers into his arm. Why was he trying to convince the guy? If he was going to talk, he should try to talk them out of here.

"That is not my problem." Zach leaned against the counter, his eyes flicking toward the door. "By the time that happens, I'll be sitting on a beach in South America, enjoying a retirement generously funded by my partner. Who you're about to meet, by the way."

Fear gripped Becky's throat. When the partner showed up, their lives could be measured in terms of minutes. *Lord, I don't want to die!* She moved a half step behind Scott, tilting her head so she could see the doorway around his shoulder.

When Zach's partner stepped through, her jaw went slack.

Leslie Stevens.

The woman's dark eyes moved as she looked from Scott to Becky, a thin smile on her face. "Now, Zach, are you giving away all my secrets?"

"I should have known." Scott sounded angry. Color stained his cheeks. "Nick was too forgiving the other night. I should have suspected he was guilty when he let me go without calling the police."

Leslie crossed the room to stand beside Zach, her eyes on Scott. "You're wrong. Nicky enjoys playing the role of big-time breeder, but he doesn't want to be bothered with the details. He's blissfully unaware of my plan, as is my baby brother, who's too dumb to know what he's helping with. Though Nicky should have had you thrown in jail for trespassing."

Becky searched Leslie's face. Where was the love she'd seen the other day? This woman's eyes glittered with a hardness that left Becky cold. "So you seduced Neal to try to convince him to go along with your scheme."

Leslie's gaze slid to her face. "No, I didn't seduce Neal." A smirk contorted her face. "I tried, but he didn't want to play. But at least my efforts kept him involved while Zach and our British friend collected the specimens they needed." She glanced sideways at her partner. "If only Zach had listened to me and tranquilized Alidor, Neal would still be alive. And that lowlife bookie would, too."

The look Scott turned on Zach was sad. "You killed Eddie Jones, too?"

"That was your fault." Scott jerked upright, and Zach nodded. "You told me about those tally sheets, and how you mentioned them to Eddie. I figured Eddie broke in and stole them to keep his name from coming up to the police. I couldn't afford to let them fall into the wrong hands. My name was probably on there right along with his."

"You're a bookmaker, too?"

His free hand waved in the air. "Hey, I'm building a

very nice retirement package." His grip tightened on the pistol. Becky's breath caught in her throat. "But Jones didn't have them."

Hugh Keller did. Becky thought of Mr. Keller's thick, muscular build. Zach was lean and fit, but he wouldn't have been a match for Mr. Keller. Poor Eddie Jones. Killed for something he had nothing to do with.

"What, the payment for cloning a champion wasn't enough?" Scott no longer sounded sad. He turned a glare on Leslie. "Two people are dead, and for what? For a crazy scheme that doesn't have a chance of succeeding."

"Oh, I *will* succeed." Leslie drew herself up and tossed her head so her dark hair flipped to her back. "I promise you, one day I'll stand in the Winner's Circle at the Derby. That blanket of roses will be on *my* horse. I'll show those high-class snobs what a true champion looks like." Dark fire glittered in her eyes. "Do you know what they called me in the owner's dining room at Keeneland? They called me an upstart. They said it loud enough for me to hear, too, those snooty women. I'll show them, one way or another."

Becky knew exactly which snooty women Leslie was talking about, at least one of them. Kaci's conversation echoed in Becky's memory. She'd called Neal's girlfriend an upstart.

A muffled thud sounded upstairs. Both Zach and Leslie looked toward the doorway, and the stairway beyond. Becky's mind raced.

"What are you going to do with us?" Her voice came out louder than she intended. They exchanged a glance.

"We can't let them go." Zach raised the pistol and pointed it at Becky's chest.

Scott stepped in front of her, shielding her from the

gun's path. "Where will it stop, Zach? Do you want to leave a trail of dead bodies all the way from Kentucky to South America?"

Leslie was staring toward the stairway. "Tenney?" she shouted. "What are you doing up there?"

Becky's nerves felt stretched to the breaking point. She grabbed Scott's belt and buried her face in his back. Her heart threatened to pound through her chest. *Lord, help us, please!*

Zach's voice grew soft, so soft she almost didn't hear it past the hammer of her pulse in her ears. "I didn't want to kill anyone. But now that it's done, I have to see it through to the end. I'm sorry, Scott. You're a good man."

Becky clutched the belt and pushed her face harder into Scott's back. This was it. Her death. Maybe Daddy would fight Chris for custody. Maybe—

"Police! Don't move. We've got the place surrounded."

Becky opened her eyes and risked a peek around Scott's back. An officer in a gray state police uniform ran into the room, another one directly on his heels. In the next instant, her protective barrier was ripped from Becky's grasp as Zach, moving so quickly he was a blur, shoved Scott's body out of the way. Scott fell to the floor. Pain shot through her scalp as Zach buried a fist in her hair. Her head jerked backward. Cold steel sent a shiver of terror through her skull as he shoved the gun into the base of her neck.

"Nobody move." His shout, inches from her ear, reverberated in her eardrum. "I swear I'll kill her."

Two figures slipped into the room, moving slowly. Detective Foster and Jeff Whitley. Her heart threatening to pound out of her chest, Becky's gaze locked on to the detective's. How could anyone look so calm in a situation like this?

Well, he didn't have a gun pressed to his skull, did he?

"Don't be stupid, Garrett," Foster said. "There are at least twenty cops around this house. You'll never get away."

Becky felt Zach's body tense. "They won't shoot me if I have a hostage."

Her gaze slid to Leslie. The brunette stood, paralyzed, her lips tight with fear as she stared at her partner.

"Let her go, Zach." Scott's voice sounded as calm as Foster's.

Becky wanted so badly to turn her head and look at him. She heard shuffling noises as he stood, but she didn't dare move.

"You know I can't do that." Zach's fingers tightened his grip on her hair.

"Come on, Zach. I know you. You don't want to hurt Becky. She's a woman. A mom."

"I don't want to," Zach whispered. "But I will if I have to. If you make me."

"I don't believe it." Scott's voice sounded closer. He was moving toward them, toward her. "You're a decent guy, Zach. You wouldn't make an orphan out of two little kids. I know you wouldn't."

The grip on Becky's hair relaxed a fraction. "Two kids?" Did his voice sound hesitant?

Becky stared straight ahead, at Jeff and Detective Foster. Foster didn't have a weapon, but Jeff's was pointed toward Zach. Toward her. She stared into his eyes, but his gaze was fixed on the man behind her.

Scott's voice was almost a whisper. "Yeah. Two boys. Little guys, around five or so. You have a brother, don't you, Zach?"

She heard a loud swallow inches behind her right ear. "You know I do. You met him a few months ago." The grip loosened more, and the gun actually moved away from her skin.

Detective Foster spoke. "You don't want to do this, Garrett. Give us the gun."

Becky felt his muscles go tense again. "Cops don't tell me what to do. I'm in control here, not you. Get out, all of you!"

A movement of his arm behind her. A flash of gray beside her head. The gun moved away from her head to point over her shoulder toward Detective Foster.

A blur to her left.

In the next instant, Becky was thrown to the floor, pain shooting simultaneously through the palm of her right hand where she landed and through her scalp as a handful of hair was ripped out. Scott landed on top of her and Zach. The gun clanged to the tiles and skittered away.

As one of the police officers dashed for the gun, Jeff and Foster ran toward her. They grabbed Zach and flipped him over on his stomach, Jeff reaching for his handcuffs.

Scott rolled away, and pulled her with him.

She was free. Relief melted her muscles as sobs clogged her throat. She was free.

Becky felt hands on her shoulders, pulling her upward. Scott, kneeling before her, lifted her up and into his arms.

She buried her face in his neck and surrendered to shuddering sobs. His arms tightened around her, hugging her close.

"You're okay now," he whispered, his breath warm on her ear. "It's over. You're safe."

After a blissful moment, Becky gave an embarrassed laugh and pulled away. "I'm sorry. I'm all right."

They got to their feet and she turned in time to see Leslie, hands cuffed behind her back, being led through the door. Zach cast one unreadable look in their direction before he, too, disappeared from sight.

Jeff and Detective Foster approached them.

The detective shook his head. "You two almost blew everything. We had Garrett under surveillance, waiting for him to lead us to his partner."

"You knew he killed Haldeman?" Scott directed his question to the detective, but kept a firm arm around Becky's waist.

Jeff answered. "We suspected, but we didn't have proof. Not until tonight, when we recovered the hoof pick from the desk drawer." He nodded at Becky. "At least one of you was smart enough to let us know what was going on."

"You took your time getting here," Becky scolded. She put a cool hand to her hot forehead. "I thought my boys were going to grow up motherless for sure."

Scott whirled on her. "You called the police. And after you promised not to!"

"I did not. I called my friend, Amber."

Her side felt warm where his hand lingered. Maybe she was giddy from her close brush with death, but she wanted to tell him right now, at this moment, how she felt. Heedless of Jeff and Detective Foster, she placed her fingers gently over Scott's heart and forced him to lock eyes with her. "I wasn't about to let the man I love walk into danger without backup."

*Gulp!* Did she just say the *L*-word? That wasn't what she'd planned to say. Blushing to the roots of her hair, she turned her head and started to stammer an explanation.

"The man you…" Scott turned her face toward him with a gentle finger beneath her chin. His gaze pierced her soul, and in the next moment Becky felt herself swept up into his strong arms once again. This time she hoped he'd never let go.

# EPILOGUE

Cars lined both sides of the two-lane country road in front of Out to Pasture. All kinds of cars, Becky noted as she walked arm in arm with Scott past a brand-new Mercedes parked behind a beat-up old farm truck. Seems everyone in that part of the state had turned out for Neal Haldeman's memorial service.

The weather could be iffy in early May, but today the sun shone in a deep-blue sky, and the coats of the Pasture's stallions gleamed in the radiance of a truly beautiful Kentucky spring day. Most of them had taken up positions as far as possible from the unusual activity going on in the grass behind the office, but Becky bit back a grin when she noticed Alidor keeping a watchful eye turned their way. She pitied the poor unsuspecting soul who dared to get too close to the testy stallion. Thank goodness the boys were home with Daddy today.

A cluster of mourners had gathered around Neal's nephew up at the front of the rows of folding chairs, most of which were already filled. Just beyond them, she glimpsed the big poster of Neal's smiling face on its easel beside the urn containing his ashes. Mr. Courtney stood off to one side, his hands gesturing widely as he spoke with a man Becky didn't know.

When they neared the chairs, a tall figure approached. Becky's hand tightened on Scott's arm. Kaci Buchanan had certainly dressed for the occasion. Her wide-brimmed hat with a thick red ribbon looked more appropriate for boxed seats at the Derby than a memorial service.

The smile she turned on Becky could have frozen hot coals. But when her gaze slid over to Scott, her cherry-colored lips widened.

"My, my, my, you would certainly dress up a Winner's Circle in that suit." Becky's teeth ground together as the heiress's gaze traveled from Scott's head to his polished black shoes. Then a shiny lip protruded. "But I hear you declined Mother's offer."

"I did." Scott's smile might have ignited a flare of jealousy in Becky, but at the same time he covered her hand on his arm and squeezed. "Lee Courtney needs me to do double duty for a while here, until he can find someone to take over at Shady Acres."

Scott's gesture did not go unnoticed. Kaci's eyes narrowed. "Then you won't be taking the head position for Lee?"

"No, I won't. I've had enough of the breeding business for a while." Scott inclined his head toward Alidor's paddock. "I'm going to stay at the Pasture and make sure these old guys enjoy their retirement."

"Well." She leaned forward and tapped his chest with a polished fingernail. "Our loss is their gain."

Her chin lifted as she caught sight of someone behind them and moved on. Becky refrained from voicing any of the less-than-polite comments that itched the tip of her tongue.

"Becky, there you are."

Fingers plucked at her sleeve, and she turned to see Isabelle Keller. Becky searched the woman's face. Grief had etched lines around her eyes, but at least she no longer exhibited signs of uncontrollable weeping.

Becky released Scott's arm to take both of Isabelle's hands in hers. "How are you holding up?"

"Okay." She squeezed Becky's fingers. "I miss him terribly, but I know I have to be strong for the baby."

Becky glanced at the people in their immediate vicinity. "Is your father here?"

She shook her head. "He had another commitment." She tilted her head toward Becky and went on in a lowered voice. "He's in a bit of trouble with the police and is doing community service. I think it's to keep him out of jail."

Becky's gaze slid to Scott's. That confirmed an elusive comment by Detective Foster when they'd asked him directly why Mr. Keller hadn't been arrested for burglary, even though he had apparently turned over the tally sheets that led them to suspect Zach Garrett of killing Neal.

At that moment, a trumpeter near the front stepped up beside the urn. It was time to begin the service. The man raised a shiny instrument to his lips and sounded the tune familiar to everyone who had anything at all to do with horse racing—the Call to Post.

As the clear notes echoed over the softly rolling hills of Kentucky bluegrass, the sound of hoofbeats thundered and the ground seemed to pulse with the pounding of powerful hooves on the turf. Every stallion at the Pasture, ears erect, began to run around their paddocks.

"Look at that." Scott turned a wide grin on Becky. "They remember."

"They're paying tribute to the man who brought them

here." She smiled up at him. "And the one who will keep them here."

He slipped an arm around her waist and pulled her close. "Both of us will keep them here. We're going to do it together, for years and years."

Her heart swelling with deep contentment, Becky allowed Scott to guide her toward a chair. There wasn't another person in the entire world with whom she'd rather spend her Out to Pasture years.

* * * * *

Dear Reader,

As I researched *Bluegrass Peril,* I enjoyed several visits to the only farm in the United States that provides a home for retired Thoroughbred stallions—Old Friends, in Georgetown, Kentucky. Though I've taken a few liberties with my fictitious farm, Out to Pasture, the terrible fate of many retired champions is distressingly real. The horses in these pages are fictitious, but many are modeled after real horses in residence at Old Friends. Like the farm in this book, Old Friends was founded in response to the brutal slaughter of the famed champion Ferdinand.

The stallions at Old Friends have their own tales to tell, and they will enchant you and steal your heart when you visit. The farm's founder, Michael Blowen, is one of the most dynamic men you'll ever meet. His love for these phenomenal equine athletes, and his passion for ensuring they enjoy their retirement years, are contagious. I hope it goes without saying that the victim in this book is totally fictitious, and bears no resemblance to the vivacious, charismatic and very much alive Michael Blowen.

If your sympathies for these horses have been aroused, I encourage you to read more about Old Friends at: *www.oldfriendsequine.com.*

Virginia Smith

## QUESTIONS FOR DISCUSSION

1 When the book opens, Becky is a young mom raising her children alone. What challenges do single parents face today? Where can they turn for help?

2 Scott falsely accuses his neighbor of wrongdoing. Have you ever accused a friend of something of which they are not guilty?

3 Becky questions whether her Christian duty requires her to reconcile with her ex-husband. How does her decision relate to the book's Scriptural foundation, Jeremiah 31:33b?

4 When he sees his daddy drinking beer, Jamie asks Becky, "Mommy, is that drugs?" How would you have answered?

5 Did Becky make the right decision in refusing to reconcile with Christopher? Why, or why not?

6 Becky is hesitant to report the identity of the mysterious "L" to the police. Why? How have your personal struggles had an impact upon your judgment?

7 When Scott discovers the missing hoof pick, he doesn't want to call the police. Why?

8 Have you ever known someone so driven by jealousy or envy that they perform unacceptable acts?

9 The killers were motivated by two different emotions. Which is the strongest motivator of human behavior—greed or jealousy?

10 What do you think should be done with retired Thoroughbred stallions?

*Powerful, engaging stories of romance, adventure and faith set in the past—when life was simpler and faith played a major role in everyday lives.*
*Turn the page for a sneak preview of*

*HOMESPUN BRIDE*
*by*
*Jillian Hart*

*Love Inspired Historical—love and faith throughout the ages*
*A brand-new line from Steeple Hill Books Launching this February!*

There was something about the young woman—something he couldn't put his finger on. He'd hardly glanced at her when he'd hauled her from the family sleigh, but now he took a longer look through the veil of falling snow.

For a moment her silhouette, her size, and her movements all reminded him of Noelle. How about that. Noelle, his frozen heart reminded him with a painful squeeze, had been his first—and only—love.

It couldn't be her, he reasoned, since she was married and probably a mother by now. She'd be safe in town, living snug in one of the finest houses in the county instead of riding along the country roads in a storm. Still, curiosity nibbled at him, and he plowed through the knee-deep snow. Snow was falling faster now, and yet somehow through the thick downfall his gaze seemed to find her.

She was fragile, a delicate bundle of wool—and snow clung to her hood and scarf and cloak like a shroud, making her tough to see. She'd been just a little bit of a thing when he'd lifted her from the sleigh, and his only thought at the time had been to get both women out of danger. Now something chewed at his memory. He couldn't quite figure out what, but he could feel it in his gut.

The woman was talking on as she unwound her niece's veil. "We were tossed about dreadfully. You're likely bruised and broken from root to stem. I've never been so terrified. All I could do was pray over and over and think of you, my dear." Her words warmed with tenderness. "What a great nightmare for you."

"We're fine. All's well that ends well," the niece insisted.

Although her voice was muffled by the thick snowfall, his step faltered. There *was* something about her voice, something familiar in the gentle resonance of her alto. Now he could see the top part of her face, due to her loosened scarf. Her eyes—they were a startling, flawless emerald green.

*Whoa, there.* He'd seen that perfect shade of green before—and long ago. Recognition speared through his midsection, but he already knew she was his Noelle even before the last layer of the scarf fell away from her face.

His Noelle, just as lovely and dear, was now blind and veiled with snow. His first love. The woman he'd spent years and thousands of miles trying to forget. Hard to believe that there she was suddenly right in front of him. He'd heard about the engagement announcement a few years back, and he'd known in returning to live in Angel Falls that he'd have to run into her eventually.

He just didn't figure it would be so soon and like this.

Seeing her again shouldn't make him feel as if he'd been hit in the chest with a cannonball. The shock was wearing off, he realized, the same as when you received a hard blow. First off, you were too stunned to feel it. Then the pain began to settle in, just a hint, and then rushing in until it was unbearable. Yep, that was the word to describe what was happening inside his rib cage. A pain worse than a broken bone beat through him.

Best get the sleigh righted, the horse hitched back up and the woman home. But it was all he could do to turn his back as he took his mustang by the bridle. The palomino pinto gave him a snort and shook his head, sending the snow on his golden mane flying.

*Yep, I know how you feel, Sunny,* Thad thought. Judging by the look of things, it would be a long time until they had a chance to get in out of the cold.

He'd do best to ignore the women, especially Noelle, and to get to the work needin' to be done. He gave the sleigh a shove, but the vehicle was wedged against the snow-covered brush banking the river. Not that he'd put a lot of weight on the Lord overmuch these days, but Thad had to admit it was a close call. Almost eerie how he'd caught them just in time. It did seem providential. Had they gone only a few feet more, gravity would have done the trick and pulled the sleigh straight into the frigid, fast waters of Angel River and plummeted them directly over the tallest falls in the territory.

Thad squeezed his eyes shut. He couldn't stand to think of Noelle tossed into that river, fighting the powerful current along with the ice chunks. There would have been no way to have pulled her from the river in time. Had he been a few minutes slower in coming after them or if Sunny hadn't been so swift, there would have been no way to save her. To fate, to the Lord or to simple chance, he was grateful.

Some tiny measure of tenderness in his chest, like a fire long banked, sputtered to life. His tenderness for her, still there, after so much time and distance. How about that.

Since the black gelding was a tad calmer now that the sound of the train had faded off into the distance, Thad re-hitched him to the sleigh but secured the driving reins to his saddle horn. He used the two horses working together to free the sleigh and get it realigned toward the road.

The older woman looked uncertain about getting back into the vehicle. With the way that black gelding of theirs was twitchy and wild-eyed, he didn't blame her. "Don't worry, ma'am, I'll see you two ladies home."

"Th-that would be very good of you, sir. I'm rather shaken up. I've half a mind to walk the entire mile home, except for my dear niece."

Noelle. He wouldn't let his heart react to her. All that mattered was doing right by her—and that was one thing that hadn't changed. He came around to help the aunt into the sleigh and after she was safely seated, turned toward Noelle. Her scarf had slid down to reveal the curve of her face, the slope of her nose and the rosebud smile of her mouth.

What had happened to her? How had she lost her sight? Sadness filled him for her blindness and for what could have been between them, once. He thought about saying something to her, so she would know who he was, but what good would that do? The past was done and over. Only the emptiness of it remained.

"Thank you so much, sir." She turned toward the sound of his step and smiled in his direction. If she, too, wondered who he was, she gave no real hint of it.

He didn't expect her to. Chances were she hardly remembered him, and if she did, she wouldn't think too well of him. She would never know what good wishes he wanted for her as he took her gloved hand. The layers of wool and leather and sheepskin lining between his hand and hers didn't stop that tiny flame of tenderness for her in his chest from growing a notch.

He looked into her eyes, into Noelle's eyes, the woman

he'd loved truly so long ago, knowing she did not recognize him. Could not see him or sense him, even at heart. She smiled at him as if he were the Good Samaritan she thought he was as he helped her settle onto the seat.

Love was an odd thing, he realized as he backed away. Once, their love had been an emotion felt so strong and pure and true that he would have vowed on his very soul that nothing could tarnish nor diminish their bond. But time had done that simply, easily, and they stood now as strangers.

\* \* \* \* \*

*Don't miss this deeply moving*
*Love Inspired Historical story about*
*a young woman in 1883 Montana who reunites*
*with an old beau and soon discovers that love*
*is the greatest blessing of all.*

*HOMESPUN BRIDE*
*by Jillian Hart*
*available February 2008*

*And also look for*
*THE BRITON*
*by Catherine Palmer*
*about a medieval lady who battles for*
*her family legacy—and finds true love.*

# REQUEST YOUR FREE BOOKS!
## 2 FREE RIVETING INSPIRATIONAL NOVELS
## PLUS 2 FREE MYSTERY GIFTS

**Love Inspired® SUSPENSE**

**YES!** Please send me 2 FREE Love Inspired® Suspense novels and my 2 FREE mystery gifts. After receiving them, if I don't wish to receive any more books, I can return the shipping statement marked "cancel." If I don't cancel, I will receive 4 brand-new novels every month and be billed just $3.99 per book in the U.S. or $4.74 per book in Canada, plus 25¢ shipping and handling per book and applicable taxes, if any*. That's a savings of 20% off the cover price! I understand that accepting the 2 free books and gifts places me under no obligation to buy anything. I can always return a shipment and cancel at any time. Even if I never buy another book from Steeple Hill, the two free books and gifts are mine to keep forever.

123 IDN EL5H  323 IDN ELQH

| | |
|---|---|
| Name | (PLEASE PRINT) |

| | |
|---|---|
| Address | Apt. # |

| | | |
|---|---|---|
| City | State/Prov. | Zip/Postal Code |

Signature (if under 18, a parent or guardian must sign)

**Order online at www.LoveInspiredSuspense.com**

**Or mail to Steeple Hill Reader Service™:**

**IN U.S.A.:** P.O. Box 1867, Buffalo, NY 14240-1867
**IN CANADA:** P.O. Box 609, Fort Erie, Ontario L2A 5X3

Not valid to current Love Inspired Suspense subscribers.

**Want to try two free books from another series?**
**Call 1-800-873-8635 or visit www.morefreebooks.com**

* Terms and prices subject to change without notice. NY residents add applicable sales tax. Canadian residents will be charged applicable provincial taxes and GST. This offer is limited to one order per household. All orders subject to approval. Credit or debit balances in a customer's account(s) may be offset by any other outstanding balance owed by or to the customer. Please allow 4 to 6 weeks for delivery.

**Your Privacy:** Steeple Hill is committed to protecting your privacy. Our Privacy Policy is available online at www.eHarlequin.com or upon request from the Reader Service. From time to time we make our lists of customers available to reputable firms who may have a product or service of interest to you. If you would prefer we not share your name and address, please check here. ☐

![Love Inspired]

When Mule Hollow rancher Nate Talbert asked for a miracle to change his reclusive life, he wasn't sure he meant Pollyanna McDonald. The widowed city woman, her eight-year-old daredevil and menagerie of unruly pets had moved next door, driving him crazy. Yet Pollyanna's son was sorely in need of a father figure. Could he be the one to help?

Look for

# Next Door Daddy

by

# Debra Clopton

**Available January**

*wherever books are sold.*

www.SteepleHill.com

Steeple Hill®

# TITLES AVAILABLE NEXT MONTH

## Don't miss these four stories in January

### FAMILY IN HIS HEART by Gail Gaymer Martin

Nick Thornton could tell Rona Meyers was a special person, so he'd offered her a much-needed job. And as he got to know her, he couldn't stop wondering if God was offering him a new beginning and a second chance at love.

### NEXT DOOR DADDY by Debra Clopton

*A Mule Hollow novel*

When rancher Nate Talbert prayed for a change to his reclusive life, he got new next-door neighbor Pollyanna McDonald. But the menagerie of pets that she and her son cared for was driving him *crazy*. Could he handle the chaos that surrounded her?

### THE DOCTOR'S BRIDE by Patt Marr

Everyone in town was trying to find Dr. Zack Hemingway a wife. Yet the one girl who caught his eye wasn't interested. Why was Chloe Kilgannon hiding from him? This doctor knew it would take some good medicine to get to the heart of the matter.

### A SOLDIER'S PROMISE by Cheryl Wyatt

*Wings of Refuge*

Pararescue jumper Joel Montgomery had the power to make a sick little boy's dream come true. He was determined to follow through even if it meant returning to a place he'd rather forget. And meeting the boy's pretty teacher made his leap of faith doubly worth the price.